KN

THE SEAMSTRESS

THE SEAMSTRESS

Aileen Armitage

This title first published in Great Britain 1999 by
SEVERN HOUSE PUBLISHERS LTD of
9–15 High Street, Sutton, Surrey SM1 1DF.
Originally published 1972 under the title
Rose Brocade and pseudonym *Aileen Quigley*.
This title first published in the U.S.A. 1999 by
SEVERN HOUSE PUBLISHERS INC of
595 Madison Avenue, New York, N.Y. 10022.

British Library Cataloguing in Publication Data

Armitage, Aileen
    The seamstress
    I.   Title
    823.9'14 [F]

ISBN 0 7278 5410 0

All situations in this publication are fictitious and
any resemblance to living persons is purely coincidental.

Printed and bound in Great Britain by
MPG Books Ltd, Bodmin, Cornwall.

For
Evelyn
and
Eric,
my parents

ONE

THE gaze of the two women met and interlocked. For a moment Garnet could not turn her head away. She felt her eyes held as if mesmerised by the blue eyes of the old woman, and an electrifying current seemed to pass from them to her own. Despite the watery paleness of the eyes, they seemed to hold an immense power, and Garnet shivered as she felt herself held in their thrall. It was not a terrifying look, but her eyes were magnetised by their intensity; then suddenly someone's head intervened and in moments Garnet had lost sight of the old crone in the seething mass of bodies in the crowd.

"He's coming!" a voice cried, and immediately Garnet forgot the old woman. The bodies around her seethed more furiously, everyone straining to see over the heads in front, to catch a glimpse of the King pass by. Garnet felt the breath squeezed out of her body by the pressing throng, and laughed invitingly to a cavalier by her side.

"Heavens! I think I shall never live to see His Majesty at this rate! Help me, I pray you!"

The cavalier needed no second invitation. Unhesitatingly he slid his arm about her waist and swung her up and clear of the massed bodies, and, forcing his broad shoulders through the crowd, he carried her at length to where the clamour was less insistent.

"There he is!" he announced with satisfaction, and by standing on tiptoe Garnet was able to catch a glimpse of the

7

dark, erect figure on horseback, waving and smiling to the crowd.

"Our bonny Black Boy!" she breathed.

"You are an admirer of His Majesty?" her cavalier enquired, and Garnet could see his grey eyes were twinkling with amusement.

"Indeed," she replied.

"I would I knew his secret," her companion retorted, "to have all women at his feet. Oh that a man should be so fortunate!"

Garnet eyed him curiously up and down. He was not unhandsome himself, this tall, fair youth with the dazzling plume in his velvet hat. A gentleman, judging by the fine lace on his sleevebands and the deferential manner in which he held his hat in his hand as he spoke to her. But it was King Charles and his company she had come this far to Hyde Park to see, and see him she would. It was not often she could persuade her employer, Madame Barin, to allow her to take the afternoon holiday and go to the Park, but today Madame had relented.

"Vairy well," she had said reluctantly in her high-pitched voice which had never lost its French accent, "if you are sure every last stitch is completed on the gowns for Mistress James. I promised the gowns faithfully for today, and you know we never fail a customer." And after running a highly critical eye over the work Garnet had laboured on by candlelight until the small hours of the morning, she had finally let her go. At the last moment her native French business acumen had seen a way to profit from the situation.

"And take good care to note the costume of the ladies in the royal retinue," she had called from the doorstep, her gaunt, grey figure contradicting the brightness of the day. "If you see any new details we have not noted, you must dress a manikin accordingly when you return."

Garnet fled, glad to agree to any extra work if only to be free for a few hours. She was conscious that she looked her best in her old **dark** green gown trimmed with the remnant of pale green silk Madame Barin had allowed her to keep. The touch of green silk set off her glossy black hair to advantage, and she walked with a jaunty air, confident of her attractions.

The young man at her side evidently appreciated them too, for without a word he slid his arm about her waist again, and drew her forward through the crowd.

"Can you see now?" he asked.

Garnet drew in a deep breath of delight. The King had passed by, and behind him rumbled a crested coach. Within its shade sat several elegant ladies, beautifully coiffured and with their faces carefully painted to enhance their features. But it was the magnificence of their gowns that caught Garnet's trained eye. It was not for nothing that she had been apprenticed to a skilled craftswoman like Madame Barin for three years.

The coach jerked to a halt just in front of them. Garnet felt a sharp pressure on her elbow, and turned to see the pale blue eyes of the old woman staring into her own again.

Momentarily a shudder ran through her. The old crone's stare was so piercing that Garnet felt as though her soul was laid naked, and tried to turn away. The old creature gripped her elbow.

"Go away from here, before it's too late," she hissed. Garnet stared at her in surprise.

"What do you mean?" she asked.

"Go away from here—there is evil afoot for you if you stay," the woman muttered.

"I don't know what you mean," Garnet retorted. "What harm is there in watching the King, I'd like to know?"

"Take no notice of her," said the young man, removing the old woman's grip from Garnet's elbow. "She's crazy. Go away, you old *crétin*. Leave us alone. We do not wish to be tainted with the plague. Go away!"

The old woman turned her gaze for a moment to the

9

young man, then blinked quickly back to Garnet. "My message is for you—not for him. It is written in your face. There is evil for you if you stay. Not today mayhap, but it will follow."

"How do you know?" asked Garnet, unable to resist the icy chill that struck into her heart.

"I do not know. Some strange power, perhaps. I've always been able to tell when sometimes I see it in a face. And it's in yours now. Go, before you repent."

Garnet heard the impatient click of the tongue from the youth at her side before the crowd started to roar with approval. She looked back at the coach. One of the beautifully dressed creatures inside was putting out a dainty foot to descend.

"What is the cause of our delay?" she was asking. "Please remove these people so that we may proceed," but Garnet heard no more. She was captivated by the magnificent gown the petulant creature was wearing, a gorgeous deep red brocade, like the velvety heart of a rose, showing off her creamy skin and gleaming gold ringlets to perfection. Moreover, Garnet noticed, there were tiny rosebuds worked intricately in the brocade, and she pitied the poor creature whose aching fingers must have laboured over it. It was magnificent—perfection. No woman on earth could wish for a more beautiful gown. Garnet's heart ached in ecstatic envy. If only she could possess a gown of such stuff!

The lady, assured of the coach's being able to re-start, climbed back inside, and in moments it had gone. Garnet turned. There was no longer any sign of the old woman who had cast a brief chill over this sunny day, but her cavalier stood attentive, casting a cool glance of appraisal over her as the crowd began to dwindle away.

"Shall we go and dine?" he asked, taking her arm with a proprietary air.

"I don't even know your name," Garnet answered with a laugh.

10

"Mine is Nick—Old Nick if you like—but in fact it is Nicholas Graveney. And yours, may I ask?"

"Garnet Appleby. Apprentice dressmaker. And no match for a gentleman," she retorted gaily. She was enjoying this. Flirtation and coquetry were fun, and a game she had been able to handle for some time now. At sixteen, one was quite adept at the game if one was attractive enough, and Garnet knew that men did indeed find her slim figure and glossy dark hair inviting.

"On the contrary, I think you would be a match for any man, King or commoner," Nicholas replied seriously. His grey eyes were regarding her thoughtfully, but somehow Garnet felt there was a coolness, a coldness even, in his look that she did not care for. As though he were cold-bloodedly assessing her and her possibilities. He had been charming enough, but she felt there was something detached, even ruthless, in his manner.

Silly girl, she told herself inwardly, he's just an adventurous youth with an eye for a pretty and equally adventurous girl, that's all. Best to shake him off now, for it was time to return to Madame Barin's, and Madame would not welcome followers to her employees. She would make short shrift of him, and no mistake, and Garnet would hear more of it later —much more.

But how to get rid of him without trouble, that was the question. She caught sight of a little old man, tottering along on a stick.

"Oh, look! A cripple—and aren't those the marks of leprosy on his skin?" she asked Nicholas with an air of innocence.

Instantly she saw Nicholas' narrow grey eyes widen in alarm.

"Where?" he said, quickly turning to look about him. Garnet took her opportunity and slipped swiftly amongst the crowd, half-crouching until she neared the paling of the Park. By then Nicholas was nowhere in sight.

Nicholas was still looking round him in agitation. The only old man he could see was a cripple, evidently an old campaigner, who had lost the use of one leg, but his skin, apart from being furrowed and weatherbeaten, bore no telltale white marks of leprosy. What was the silly girl thinking about? He looked about for her, expecting to see the gleam of the sun on that glorious blue-black hair, but she was gone. Damn the wench! Where was she?

He pushed on through the laughing, chattering people, but she was nowhere in sight. Dammit, she'd given him the slip. Why the devil, then, had she bothered to give him all those coy, come-hither glances and leave to hold her close? Why indeed, if she hadn't expected the normal consequences and a gold piece at the end of the afternoon?

Ah well, Nicholas reflected philosophically, perhaps it was as well. She was a lively, no doubt energetic filly, and doubtless by the evening he would have been so fatigued by his efforts that he'd have been in no fit state to show his best face at the Wreckers' Club tonight. And as one of the leading members of the Wreckers, it behoved him to appear always enthusiastic and indefatigable.

And, in any case, that child—what was her name?— Garnet, was but a sewing-apprentice. Hardly suitable for a gentleman to be seen with, however pretty, so he could never have taken her to the Club with him. And since the meeting was to be at Hugo's house tonight, Hugo could be relied upon to produce a string of attractive fillies, all of them guaranteed active and free from contagion. It would never do to get a dose of the clap, like that silly fellow Roger. One could never be too careful. No, perhaps it was as well that he had lost the girl.

Still, it was a pity, he reflected. He hadn't even had to make the opening gambit with her. He sighed as he saw again in his mind's eye the slender figure and silken hair, but dismissed the tempting thought from his mind and set off towards home, to prepare for the evening's fun.

12

Garnet sat hunched on a stool by the kitchen fire, absent-mindedly clutching a mug of ale in one hand and nibbling at a piece of bread.

"Cheese?" asked Nancy, the newest apprentice to Madame Barin's establishment.

"Mmmm? No thank you," murmured Garnet.

"What are you dreaming about, Garnet?"

"The procession. The King and his courtiers."

"Did they wear beautiful clothes? Did Madame have you dress a manikin?"

"There was no need. There weren't any new details of style, only the most wonderful stuffs I have ever seen. Oh, Nancy, there was the most beautiful red brocade I ever saw in my life! Such a gown I swear I shall own for myself one day, or my name isn't Garnet Appleby."

Nancy giggled. "Brocade for a sewing maid? You don't half fancy yourself, don't you?" Seeing Garnet made no reply, she went on, "Madame says you fancy yourself a cut above the others here. She says you put on airs and think yourself the lady, but I don't find you at all haughty."

She waited, kneeling by Garnet and looking up at her appealingly. Garnet felt sorry for the child, barely thirteen and with her fingers already raw and sore from all the work Madame Barin had inflicted on her.

"I fancy Madame is perhaps a little jealous, Nancy. She knows something of my history and I think she gains a certain malicious pleasure from having someone better born than herself working for her."

Nancy's eyes gleamed. "Then you are a lady," she said with satisfaction.

"Hardly a lady, but my father was quite wealthy until the time of the troubles. Then Cromwell stripped him of his lands and money on account of father's loyalty to the Crown. By the time His Majesty was restored to the throne, father had died and my mother was left alone and defenceless with a young child to care for."

"And so your mother had to put you to work?"

"Not then—I was too young. She decided the best protection she could give us both was to remarry, so when a certain merchant, middle-aged but esteemed, proposed marriage to her, she accepted. She felt certain that with his business sense he would husband carefully the little resources she had left."

"But he didn't?" Nancy breathed, guessing the outcome.

"Not he!" Garnet replied sharply. "Young though I was, I realised my mother was unhappy. Slowly I saw her fade and droop, like an autumn flower. She never spoke of it till she lay on her deathbed, and then she warned me, so gently but so firmly, that I must look to myself, for no one else would. Reginald Baskcomb had gambled away her little inheritance and was growling that there was no more. His own business was crumbling fast, and there would be no security for me once she was gone."

"How old were you then, Garnet?"

Garnet looked at the girl. "About your age, Nancy. Near enough thirteen."

"And where is your stepfather now? Is he still alive?"

"Oh, yes. He is here, in London, not far away. I go to visit him sometimes when Madame allows me to have a short holiday."

She did not tell Nancy of the misery of the five years she and her docile mother had suffered at the hands of Reginald Baskcomb, from the time she was a small child until the time her mother died.

In those years Baskcomb was never known to say a kind word, neither to his wife and stepdaughter nor to his servants. A quick blow or a cruel word came far more easily to his fiery nature than kindness. More than once Garnet had had to watch her gentle mother flinch while Baskcomb vented his anger on her because her money was dwindling. Garnet had burned with rage on her mother's behalf, and she would have flown at him with her fingernails outstretched but for her

14

mother, who bore all his raging in quiet submission and bade Garnet do the same.

"Do not seek revenge, my sweet," she had murmured gently to her daughter. "Rather bear all and bide your time. One day you will be free." So Garnet had waited impatiently for freedom, for herself and for her mother, but her mother was never to taste it. Worn down by Baskcomb's constant harassing and demands, she faded away. Only on her deathbed had she permitted herself the disloyalty of speaking against her husband, warning Garnet to go away, for at thirteen she was old enough to fend for herself.

So Garnet had left, and Baskcomb had been so befuddled with drink, drowning his disappointment, that he had scarcely noticed. Now, settled for the last three years in Madame Barin's house, Garnet had visited her stepfather only as often as duty demanded.

Nor did she tell Nancy that these visits were infrequent and usually unhappy occasions. Reginald Baskcomb had no use for his stepdaughter unless she brought him a little money to help provide yet another evening of gambling and heavy drinking, and as Garnet earned little beyond her keep, he scowled whenever he saw her on his doorstep.

All this Garnet did not tell Nancy. Perchance the child would repeat it to Madame, who would find in it fresh fodder for her gossiping tongue.

"Come, 'tis time we were abed, Nancy," she said instead, and helped the girl lay out her pallet and blanket on the floor. Garnet herself was more fortunate, as the senior apprentice, and she crawled between the blankets on her truckle bed gratefully.

Soon all the house was quiet save for the crackling of the dying log fire as the embers hissed and settled down in the grate. Nancy began to snore, but Garnet lay awake, going over in her mind the events of the day.

She had enjoyed her outing to the Park and the attention of the handsome young man Nicholas. It was flattering to

15

one's vanity to have such a fine dandy paying court, if only for a brief half-hour. She laughed to herself as she recalled how she had given him the slip, then suddenly she checked herself.

A pair of intense blue eyes stared at her out of the mists of memory. The old woman and her warning. What on earth had the old witch tried to warn her of?

Something in the Park would lead to evil for Garnet, she had said. What had Garnet seen that might forebode evil? Only the handsome gentleman she would probably never see again and the ladies in the coach—oh, and especially the fair young creature in the magnificent rose brocade gown. What harm could there possibly be in that?

Yawning sleepily, Garnet dismissed the old woman's warning as the ramblings of an old dotard. She turned over in the narrow bed and, picturing herself stepping daintily from a coach in a rose brocade gown, she went contentedly to sleep.

TWO

THE following day Garnet was sewing in the rear of the house, the chamber behind the one in which Madame received her clients and discussed their requirements with them. Nancy squatted close by, wincing every now and again as she pricked herself on her sore fingertips.

Garnet sewed swiftly on, her mind busy with her own thoughts. She had a strange, tingling feeling that today something was going to happen. She could give no name to the feeling or guess what kind of event she foresaw, only a certain, inevitable presentiment that something would befall.

She considered the possibilities. Customers of so many kinds came to Madame's establishment that one could never be sure who might call today. There could be a merchant's daughter, eagerly examining materials for her wedding trousseau, with a dictatorial mother countermanding her every order. There could be a stout matron, insisting Madame had got her measurements all wrong or it was the gown which had been sewn too tightly, and a flurried argument would ensue, which usually ended with Madame flouncing from the chamber and sending Garnet in to soothe the vexed customer.

Or it could be a merchant's wife ordering a new Sunday-best gown, having brought her husband with her to approve her choice of material and design. And Garnet was accustomed to seeing the gentleman's interested stare across the top of his wife's bent head, directed at herself. She did not discourage the gleam in his eye, whoever he was. It was flattering

17

to one's vanity to note a gentleman's approval. And so long as Madame Barin did not notice, where was the harm? Occasionally, however, Madame did notice, and afterwards Garnet would be subjected to a long and fiery tirade about a servant knowing her place, and her duty to discourage such attentions and attend to her work.

Nancy suddenly exclaimed sharply and Garnet was brought back to the present. "Drat this damn fustian!" Nancy said bitterly. "Who on earth would choose such vile stuff for a gown?"

"Let me see," said Garnet kindly. The child was clumsy and erratic in her stitching yet, so she unpicked and resewed the seam for her adroitly before Madame returned. "There," she said, handing the length of stuff back to her. "Keep your stitches small and neat, and push the needle with your thimble, not your finger."

Nancy smiled gratefully. Garnet had just taken up her own sewing again when Madame Barin bustled into the room.

"*Bon Dieu!*" she exclaimed, fanning herself angrily with a scrap of material. "Some people are so difficult to please! Mistress Trubshawe fancies she will have blue this time—or shall it be red? Silk, she thinks, for a change—or possibly satin. She has chosen three times already, then hesitated and changed her mind again. What am I to do for such a client?"

She paced up and down the chamber, ruffling the hitherto calm atmosphere with her vexation. "Every bolt of cloth I possess has been unrolled for her, and still she cannot decide, so I have left her to ponder alone for a time. Go you in to her, Garnet, and see if you can help her make up her silly mind."

Garnet laid aside her sewing carefully and went through to the outer chamber. Mistress Trubshawe, plump and amiable, stood by the latticed window with a troubled frown marring the smooth whiteness of her forehead.

"Can I help you, Mistress?" asked Garnet, standing politely by the door.

"Ah, Garnet, if you would, please." Mistress Trubshawe's face lit up at the sight of the girl. "You know what suits me better than I do myself, and, though I hesitate to say it, Madame Barin does not help me at all. I become so flustered when I feel her eyes on me, willing me to make up my mind and get it over and done with."

"She is a fine craftswoman," said Garnet loyally.

"Indeed, I know it," replied the older woman, "but she has no patience with me. I know the style I want," she said, holding out the manikin she held clutched in her hand, "but not the colour. It is as my husband says, I fear. I need someone to make decisions for me."

"Come, then," said Garnet gently, "what shall it be? Which colour do you prefer of all colours?"

"Oh, red," breathed the other ecstatically, "but I fear lest it may not suit me."

"On the contrary," said Garnet, sizing up her fair skin and light gold hair beginning to turn grey. "I think it would suit you admirably. An excellent choice, if I may say so."

Deftly, Garnet unrolled and displayed one bolt of red cloth after the other, but Mistress Trubshawe fingered them all in turn and still she hesitated. "Alas," she said, "I cannot decide. There is none which truly appeals to me—none which I feel is really *me*, if you know what I mean. Oh, what am I to do?"

Garnet felt sorry for the pale creature, pathetic despite her size. Suddenly she remembered that Madame Barin was expecting new deliveries of cloth.

"If the ship is in port, there will soon be further bolts for you to choose from," she told Mistress Trubshawe. "I suggest you delay your choice until then. We will send word to you as soon as they come."

Mistress Trubshawe was delighted to be able to postpone the terrifying moment of decision, and she left the house smiling happily. Madame Barin, however, was not so pleased at the outcome.

19

"She will be the happier when she finds exactly the stuff she wants," Garnet protested in self-defence.

"She'll never know what she wants when she sees it," Madame retorted sharply. "You should have pressed her for an order while you could. You will never make a business woman, you stupid child."

Her irritation was soon dissipated when the bolts of new cloth were delivered to her shop that same afternoon. Nancy was dispatched post-haste to Mistress Trubshawe's to tell her the good news and to invite her to return and make her choice.

"In the meantime you may help me unpack and display the stuffs," Madame told Garnet. Both women exclaimed with pleasure at the pretty materials they unwrapped: damson taffeta, cinnamon velvet, tangerine satin, and the most luxurious brocades of emerald green and dusky brown.

Garnet held up the green brocade. "Just imagine this over a kirtle of paler green and trimmed with silver lace," she said to Madame. "Would it not be a splendid gown, fit for a lady?"

Madame clicked her tongue. "Too fine by far for most of my clients, I regret, merchants' wives and the like. But no doubt it would suit a lady of your fine manners," she added with a mocking, tight-lipped attempt at a smile.

Garnet did not answer. Her gaze had fallen on a much smaller roll of cloth than the others, still partly wrapped and with just a corner extruding from its wrappings. A deep, rich red shining material, and was that not a minute rosebud she could see embroidered upon it? She dropped the green brocade and picked up the smaller roll instantly.

As she uncovered the red cloth, her breath caught in her throat. It was the same magnificent deep rose brocade the lady in the coach had been wearing—the very same. Garnet could not help the sigh of satisfaction and desire that issued from her lips. She held the stuff close to her throat, savouring the sensation of luxury.

Madame Barin looked at the cloth critically. "Mmm, pretty enough, but barely enough of it for one amply cut gown, I fancy. With careful cutting, however, we might manage to accommodate Mistress Trubshawe, if she takes a fancy to it."

Garnet felt a stab of disappointment. Of course the material must be used for a customer, but the prospect of losing it, especially to a plump, dowdy creature like Mistress Trubshawe, was heartbreaking. As Madame said, the entire roll would be used up in making a gown for her.

But when Mistress Trubshawe reappeared and beamed happily at the sight of the deep rose brocade, vowing that this was what she had been seeking, Garnet could not begrudge her the one gown she knew she would feel happy and confident in wearing. Madame Barin, her equanimity restored, measured and cut swiftly after Mistress Trubshawe had left.

"One week from today it must be ready," she told Garnet. "So waste no time in seeing to it." Garnet gathered up the pieces and took them to her corner. Nancy's eyes grew wide in admiration.

"Oooh! What a lovely colour," she sighed. "Oh, Garnet, that would suit you beautifully, you a lady an' all."

Yes, thought Garnet, it was destined for a young girl, with dark hair, not a faded, middle-aged creature. Sadly she tacked the pieces of the skirt together, luxuriating in the feel of the fine texture. She sewed on with concentration until the candles were lit and supper laid, then again after the dishes had been cleared away.

Late that night, when everyone was asleep, Garnet had all the main pieces of the gown assembled. She held it high to inspect it, and then noticed that there was still a piece on the floor. She laid the gown down and picked up the piece curiously. It was a left-over remnant, about a yard square, a tribute to Madame's skilful cutting.

Just about enough for a neckerchief, thought Garnet, and,

21

folding it cornerways, she draped the rustling piece about her shoulders. Then, taking up the candle, she stepped over the prostrate figure of Nancy and went through to the outer chamber, where she tried to see her reflection by candlelight in the glass doors of the corner cupboard.

Upstairs, Madame Barin lay awake, mentally going over the yardage and price of the new stuffs. What was that? She sat upright in bed. A scuffling sound, a mouse perhaps, or one of the girls downstairs? Best to make sure, in case one of those thoughtless creatures had left the door unlatched.

She rose quickly and struck a light for her candle, then quietly glided down the stairs. In the rear room Nancy lay snoring on the floor, her mouth agape. Disgusting, thought Madame, a revolting sight and, moreover, distinctly unhealthy. Who in his right mind would want to absorb more of this pestilential London air than he could help?

She looked across to Garnet's bed, and saw with surprise that it was empty. Was the girl still sewing, then? No, there were her needles and thimble in the corner. Where the devil was she, then?

She stepped over the sleeping Nancy and flung open the door to the outer chamber. Garnet, humming a little tune to herself, was pirouetting about, candle in hand and with a piece of Mistress Trubshawe's red brocade about her shoulders. She was so absorbed in admiring her mirrored reflection that she did not notice Madame's entrance.

So that was it. The vain creature still had pretensions of being the lady, did she? Just because the family had 'had some money once, but now her father was dead and her feckless mother had somehow lost it all before she, too, died. Well, it was time she learnt her place. Others besides her had been forced to come down in the world, thought Madame bitterly, and had learnt to work hard for a living. So must she, pert little piece.

Garnet stopped suddenly as she caught sight of Madame's

22

taut face, and pulled the brocade from her neck, holding it behind her.

"It is too late for pretence, my girl, I have caught you," Madame said in a staccato voice. The impudence of the girl, trying to hide the material she was undoubtedly planning to keep for herself. "Give that to me."

Garnet handed over the brocade without a word. That was evidence in itself of her deceit, Madame thought savagely. She could not help it; this was the opportunity she 'had been waiting for, to pour out all her dislike and resentment of the impertinently lovely, mild-mannered creature who so obviously considered herself far above her mistress. Madame had noted with disfavour how men callers to the shop, accompanying their wives or daughters, obviously eyed this pretty chit with a more than passing interest. And what was even more hurtful, Madame was reluctant to admit even to herself.

Master Bolitho, the plump and amiable widower merchant whom Madame was pleased to entertain in her parlour ever since he had kindly offered to advise her on the purchase of new stuffs, had taken to calling more frequently of late. Madame's 'heart had begun to flutter hopefully, until she realised that while Master Bolitho spoke to her, his eyes were following Garnet, an eager gleam in them that Madame had hoped was intended for herself. The audacious girl's grace and rounded figure had drawn Madame's attention unwillingly to her own bony angularity, and she hated Garnet for the lively warmth that negated her own faded charms.

So she took the opportunity now to let all her pent-up resentment burst forth, accusing Garnet of laziness and deceit, of almost losing her a valued customer, and finally she brought out her trump card.

"And to cap it all, I find you stealing from me—me, your benefactress, who taught you all the skill you know! What way is this to repay all my kindness to you? But now my eyes are opened to your duplicity, Mistress Garnet. I will harbour you in my house no longer. Who knows 'how you might

23

corrupt the younger ones like Nancy? Out of my house you go, you hear me? No, do not attempt to defend your actions. In the morning you will leave, and there is an end to it!"

She turned and flounced angrily out of the room, flinging the piece of brocade on to the pile of sewing materials in the back room as she passed. Justice had been done, she felt. She would sleep more peacefully tonight.

Garnet looked after the retreating figure, her emotions a confusion of anger and bewilderment. Madame Barin had given her no chance to explain, but had immediately jumped to an unjustifiable conclusion. How dare she call Garnet a thief! Resentment blazed inside her. She had served Madame faithfully and to the best of her ability, and this was how she was repaid. Thrown out in disgrace, homeless and friendless, and probably penniless, too, for it was unlikely Madame would pay due wages to a thief!

Garnet went back into the inner chamber. Surprisingly, Nancy was still sleeping soundly despite the noise of Madame's outburst. Garnet cursed in vexation as she stubbed her toe on the foot of the truckle bed; then she caught sight of the remnant Madame had flung aside.

She picked it up and fingered its supple texture thoughtfully. It was so beautiful, so luxurious. She gathered together her few belongings to tie them into a bundle, ready to leave at first light. Still the piece of rose brocade was in her hand. She was reluctant to let it go.

Dammit, she thought, I've been branded as a thief, so I might as well earn the name! Defiantly she stuffed the piece into her bundle and tied it tightly. Now it's mine, she thought, and one day I shall have that gown I dream of. I swear I will, by all that's holy.

At dawn she awoke. Nancy was no longer asleep on the floor, but Garnet could hear Madame Barin scolding her roundly in an upstairs chamber. No doubt she was telling her of Garnet's downfall, and warning her lest the same fate should befall her.

Garnet rose and dressed, then putting on her heavy cloak and taking up her bundle she unlatched the outer door and let herself out into the street. There was no point in provoking a further scene with Madame. Out on the mist-damp cobblestones she turned and looked back at the house. A small tear-stained face was looking out from an upstairs window. It was Nancy. Garnet gave a quick wave and blew her a kiss, then ran swiftly down the street and away.

Although it was still early, the narrow London streets were already filled with labourers on their way to work, and country farmers jogging into the city with their day's produce for sale aboard their wooden-wheeled carts, clattering and jolting over the cobblestones. All were intent on their business and none had time to spare to quip with the pretty, dark girl hurrying on her way.

Half an hour later she approached the ramshackle old house where Reginald Baskcomb lived. It had been an imposing residence once, but Baskcomb's preoccupation with acquiring sufficient money to live on and gamble with had left no room in his thoughts for the state of his house. It was a roof over his head, a haven to retreat to, and as long as it sheltered him, its appearance was of little consequence.

Garnet had no wish to impose on Baskcomb, for she knew he cared naught for her, but where else could she go? She approached the front entrance hesitantly and rang the bell.

No answer came. Of course, Baskcomb was no longer able to employ servants, his fortunes were so low. Was he even at home? Thoughtfully, Garnet went round to the rear of the house, and saw with regret how overgrown and neglected the once-pretty lawns and flowerbeds had become. Her mother would have wept to see the state of her beloved herb garden now.

The garden door pushed open at her touch. Garnet went

in. The house everywhere betrayed the same neglect and confusion as the garden. At the door of the study, she stopped. Deep rumbling snores penetrated the heavy oak door. Turning the knob, Garnet went in, and stood just inside, surveying the scene.

Reginald Baskcomb lay with his head and arms sprawled across the long table, his mouth open as he gurgled, and empty flagons and overturned tankards surrounding him. The air was heavy and oppressive, with the foetid, sickly smell of sour ale and tobacco smoke. Garnet crossed the chamber and flung open the heavy drapes at the window and opened the casement. The light breeze that cut into the foul air roused Baskcomb from his torpor.

"What in hell's name . . .?" he began, lurching unsteadily to his feet, then stopping to clutch his forehead. "Oh, my head!" he moaned, and reached for one of the flagons on the table. Discovering it empty, he cursed again, then blinked slowly to clear his brain, trying to focus on the dim figure by the window.

"Who's that?" he snarled. "How did you get into my house?"

The figure moved closer. "Garnet," she said.

That fool of a girl. What was she doing here?

"The door was open, so I came in," she went on.

Stop talking, Baskcomb thought. It hurts like hell. Then a happy thought came into his mind—perhaps she had brought money. He looked at her hopefully. He could certainly use whatever she had, however little. Not only were the flagons and the larder empty, but his gambling creditors were becoming so pressing that he would have to find money somewhere soon or be forced to flee London.

"What brings you here, child?" he asked as gently as his aching throat could manage. Best to put on some show of politeness. She took off her cloak and put it on a chair.

"I was dismissed from Madame Barin's establishment."

What was that? Did he hear that small, cool voice

26

correctly? Had the chit the nerve to come here and tell him she had lost her position? Reginald Baskcomb felt the hot glow of anger beginning to rise from somewhere near his stomach and mount into his fogged brain.

"What for?" he rasped.

"She accused me of stealing a piece of cloth."

Baskcomb waited to hear no more. The hot glow reached his brain and exploded into a myriad fiery sparks, and he reached for his riding crop, somewhere among the litter on the table.

Garnet stood, awaiting the reproaches she felt sure would come, but she was unprepared for the sudden attack. The sting of the crop as it cut into her shoulder took her breath away, and she was too stunned to cry out.

Her lack of reaction seemed to madden Baskcomb all the more. His face purple with rage, he rained blow after blow on her, shouting and cursing, and his fury seemed to reach a crescendo when he struck her with his fist, sending her crashing into the marble fireplace.

Garnet lay inert, stunned and seared with pain. Through a red mist she saw Reginald Baskcomb's face, paler now and wide-eyed with fright, bending over her. Then he suddenly backed away, dropping his riding crop on the floor, and stumbled from the room.

For a time Garnet lay still; then, as the pain receded a little, she struggled to sit up. It was an agonising process, and she could not help wincing and moaning with the effort. Bascomb had not even waited to hear her explanation, so little he cared about her. All he was concerned about was the loss of her little income. Savagely she muttered to herself about his selfishness and greed.

"I should never have come here," she muttered angrily. "I should have known better. But I know now. Never again will I set foot in this house, or attempt to see him. It is as my mother said, I must make my own way in the world."

She rose stiffly. Pain seared through her limbs, but she was

27

determined to get out of this house as quickly as she could. She picked up her bundle from where it had fallen on the hearth. The pathetic little parcel had come apart during Baskcomb's attack on her, and the piece of rose brocade was lying apart on the floor.

Garnet lifted the remnant and cradled it to her for a moment before putting it back in the bundle. "My rose brocade," she murmured softly, like a mother to her sleeping child. "No one in the world cares about me now. It is for me to make what I can from life, and by God I will. The day will come, I swear it, when I shall wear rose brocade every day, and I don't care who I have to trample on to achieve it. No one shall ever treat me cheaply again."

Thus Garnet's resentment against the world at large crystallised into determination, and, taking up her cloak and bundle, she left Reginald Baskcomb's house for the last time.

THREE

GARNET wandered through the streets aimlessly, her mind too much in a turmoil to notice her aching shoulders and back. She crossed the bridge from Southwark towards Blackfriars, seeing but not registering the swirling waters of the Thames eddying as they neared the arches.

Towards midday a few raindrops spattered her throbbing cheekbone. She looked up, and realised the sun had gone and a heavy fall of rain was imminent. She quickened her footsteps, and then slackened again. To what end was she hurrying? Where could she go?

She realised at the same time that her stomach was hollow and aching, and that she had as yet eaten nothing this day. That settled it. She counted out her few coins and calculated that she had sufficient money either to eat a sound meal or to buy a bed in some tavern for the night, and the plaintive state of her stomach left her in no doubt which it was to be.

Rain was falling in earnest as she covered the now slippery cobblestones to the nearest inn. As she crossed the inn yard, a coach drew up and a lively party descended, chattering and laughing. Gaudily dressed women, shrieking and giggling, were handed down by elegant dandies in frills and silver lace.

"Come, my lovely," one fop in lavender silk was saying to a simpering, painted girl. "Cheesecake and a flagon of Canary wine to begin with, will that suit you?" He began to usher all the women towards the inn door.

"Come, my beauties, hurry out of the rain," he called to them. "We must keep you hale and hearty if you are to perform well at the theatre tonight."

He turned and put a protective arm around Garnet. "Come now, make haste," he said, and then Garnet saw his eyes light up.

"She is not with us," the painted girl remonstrated.

The man hesitated. "My apologies, mistress," he said, withdrawing his arm slowly. "I mistook you for another of my actress lady friends. But you are welcome to join our party."

Garnet saw the girl's eyes narrow. "Thank you, sir, but I must be on my way," she replied, dropping a bob curtsey, and she hastened from the inn yard before a quarrel should break out. Actresses were renowned for their fiery temperaments and jealous natures, and it would not do to provoke a street brawl with one of them. Her hunger must wait.

The rain had changed to an insistent drizzle as Garnet turned the corner into a narrow, deserted street lined with shops. She walked along the pavement, her hood drawn close against the rain, scanning the signboards on the far side of the street for another eating place.

Her attention was caught by a movement across the road. A small boy, little more than a toddler, was easing himself gently down the steep steps of a shop front. He looked up as he reached the pavement, and smiled across at Garnet, his dark eyes agleam with amusement. A rumble from the far end of the street developed into a noisy clatter as a heavy coach hastened towards them. Garnet saw the child hold out his hands towards her and start to cross the street, smiling as he came.

"Go back!" she cried, but the boy came on. Without thinking, Garnet dropped her bundle and ran at him, just as the coach lumbered on to them, snatching him into her arms and throwing herself into the far gutter all in one movement. She rolled over with him in her arms and felt the breath of air as the horse's hooves missed her head by inches.

She lay in the gutter, stunned for a moment. Then with relief she felt the child, still held tight in her arms, move and whimper. He sat up and looked at her reproachfully with huge brown eyes.

Running footsteps approached them.

"Daniel! Daniel, my boy!"

Garnet looked up into a pair of brown eyes the exact replica of the child's, but these were wide with anxiety. A man, tall and lean and soberly dressed, was bending over them.

"Are you hurt?" he asked anxiously. Garnet made to stand up, and felt his firm grip under her arm helping her.

"Thank you, no. We are both unharmed," she began to say, but the man was already tenderly holding and inspecting the toddler. Satisfied that the child was unhurt, he turned to Garnet again.

"You saved my son from almost certain death," he said. "I saw it all from the window. I can never thank you enough, mistress."

"There is no need . . ." Garnet's voice tailed away. She felt suddenly faint and dizzy. Hunger, no doubt. It was already late afternoon and she had not yet eaten.

"You are hurt!" the man exclaimed. Garnet saw his gaze was on her arms, where the cloak had fallen back, and he was looking at the bruises Baskcomb had inflicted on her.

"No, truly!" she said, but she felt herself swaying again. The man took her elbow firmly and, leading the boy by the other hand, he guided her towards the steps where she had first seen the child.

Garnet was aware of passing through the doorway into a shop, then into a rather gloomy chamber behind, where the man settled her into a chair. She began to feel a little better.

"Let me see," he said, unfastening the clasp at her throat and folding back her cloak. "These are terrible bruises," he commented, "but I have good unguents which will soothe them. But first a bowl of broth, I think." He hastened away

31

and left the boy playing on the floor at her feet. The child smiled up at her.

"Nice lady," he said.

Garnet laughed. "And you're nice, too," she said. "What is your name?"

The boy thought for a moment. "Daniel," he announced finally. "Daniel hungry. Daniel want broth."

The man returned with bowls of broth and some hunks of rye bread. "Eat," he said to Garnet, "and we'll talk later." He broke bread into a bowl of broth for the child, and helped him to spoon it.

Garnet cradled the bowl between her hands on her lap. The smell of the fresh soup was mouth-watering, and after a moment she dipped her spoon in it and ate ravenously. The man watched appreciatively and smiled.

"You are very kind, sir," Garnet said as she handed him back the empty bowl. "I was famished."

"My name is Matthew, and it is I who am indebted to you," he said quietly. "In return for my son's life, anything I have is yours. May I know the name of my benefactress?"

"Garnet Appleby."

"Garnet." He savoured the name. It sounded beautiful to Garnet's ears, spoken in that low, resonant voice. "Let me take your wet cloak, Garnet Appleby, and dry it out for you." He took it and draped it by the fire. "Where do you live, Garnet?"

Garnet hung her head. What could she reply? Neither Madame Barin's address nor Reginald Baskcomb's were her home now.

Matthew was watching her closely. "Have you no home, child?"

Garnet shook her head slowly. The idle thought crossed her mind that it was strange he called her child. He could not be more than in his middle twenties himself, barely ten years her senior.

He rose and took the bowls back to the kitchen; Garnet

could hear him clattering dishes, and after some time he returned. "Garnet," he said, standing by the door, "have you any experience of running a house? Would you consider taking employment here as my housekeeper?"

Garnet looked at him in surprise. If Daniel was his son, then where was his wife? Wasn't she capable of keeping house for him satisfactorily? Or was he simply offering her a home and employment out of gratitude, and not because he had need of her services?

"Well?" he asked again, seeing she remained silent. "Can you sew, cook and clean and wash? Or does the prospect not appeal to you?"

Garnet looked up. "I can do all those things, and more, but I wonder whether you truly need me."

It was Matthew's turn to look surprised. "I would not ask if I had no need of you," he said. "And, moreover, I should like to keep you here a time, to keep an eye to you. Let me see your bruises," he added, coming closer. There was a small pot in his hand, and he smoothed the contents of it over Garnet's arms and shoulders. His touch was gentle and reassuring, and his dark eyes sorrowful as he saw the extent of her bruises.

"Dear heaven," he murmured, "to think my carelessness was the cause of all this! I took my eyes from the boy but a moment, to see to the broth, and the little mischief must have unlatched the door by himself while my attention was diverted."

He looked across to the boy, who was playing happily on the floor now with a piece of string and a playful kitten. "As soon as I missed him, I ran through to the shop, and there, from the window, I saw your courageous action, Garnet. I shall be for ever beholden to you. Daniel is all I have."

His eyes grew soft as he looked at the boy, then he put the pot of balm away and stood up.

"But, gratitude apart, I would have you stay if, as I suppose, you have no home and no employment, because I

33

have need of a woman's hand. I am a widower, and since my wife died I find it difficult to attend to business and to a house and child as well." He paused, then added quietly, "I would be grateful for your help, for then I could devote more time to my shop."

Garnet hesitated. She liked this tall, quiet man and his child, and she surely had need of a home and employment. But she had not told Matthew of the real cause of her bruises. He had assumed they were caused by the horse—would it be deceit on her part to keep her tongue silent and accept his offer?

Matthew left the chamber, and in a moment he reappeared carrying her bundle. "I presume these are your belongings?" he said. "I saw the bundle still lying on the pavement."

"It is all I possess," laughed Garnet.

"Will you unpack?" Matthew asked.

Garnet looked into his dark eyes. He was inviting her again to stay.

"Thank you—yes."

His serious face melted into a smile. "Daniel and I are content," he said.

That evening she sat in the small bedchamber into which Matthew had shown her. He had apologised for its drab and unaired state, but Garnet determined that tomorrow she would begin in earnest her work as housekeeper. The entire house was in a similar state of dustiness and disorder, but, as Matthew had said, all it required was a woman's hand. The furnishings were of good quality, but sadly in need of soap and polish. Tomorrow she would set about bringing the sparkle back to the house.

Before settling down to sleep, she peeped into the little chamber where she had seen Matthew put his young son to bed. By the light of her candle she saw his little face, eyes closed now, and a chubby little fist gripping the cradle rail in his sleep. He seemed no worse for the accident, she noted with relief.

She slipped between the linen sheets of her own bed. They felt somewhat damp, but it was luxury to have sheets at all. Tomorrow she would thoroughly air them. Sheets, she thought, and a real high bed! As she doused the candle she reflected that her first day's adventures alone had not ended badly. A home, a new position, and a pleasant employer—life was beginning to take on a kinder shape than hitherto. Like Matthew and Daniel, she too was content.

Morning dawned bright with sunshine, all sign of yesterday's rain vanished. Matthew had already eaten breakfast when Garnet came downstairs, and Daniel, still in his nightgown, was feeding his to the kitten.

"I must lay out the shop stall," Matthew said, rising to leave. "Serve yourself, Garnet, and call me if you cannot find aught you require."

Garnet ate her breakfast with Daniel, persuading the boy to eat some of his food himself. Then, when she had washed and dressed him, she set about finding some beeswax and soap to begin cleaning. Daniel helped cheerfully, running before her to open presses and drawers. From time to time Matthew peeped round the door to see that all was well.

The day passed quickly for Garnet. In the evening a succulent smell of roasting meat drew Matthew to the kitchen where Garnet sat with Daniel. The child was gurgling with delight at the roast quince over which she was spooning cream for him. Impatiently, he took the spoon from her and devoured the soft quince greedily. Matthew smiled and stretched himself out on a chair.

"It is good to have such an appetising smell in my kitchen once more," he said.

"You must be hungry," Garnet said, rising from her stool. "Let me serve you." She felt Matthew's eyes follow her as she basted the joint once more before lifting it on to a chafing dish.

After the roast, Matthew ate with obvious relish the deliciously light and fluffy apple tansy Garnet had prepared.

35

It gave her great pleasure to see how Matthew enjoyed her cooking, and her pleasure was heightened yet more when he finally pushed his plate away, leaned back in his chair, and said, "It was a fortunate day for me indeed when you came to Cheveril Street, Garnet. Not only did you save Daniel, but you cook like an angel, too. And my house has never gleamed more brightly." He looked about him at the scrubbed flagstone floor and well-burnished copperware.

Garnet flushed with pleasure. It was many a long day since she had been praised for her labours. Madame Barin had never been one to give unstintingly of her praise, but, on the contrary, had been quick to find fault.

It gave Garnet much pleasure in the next few days to polish all the handsome, solid furniture in the house, to light fires and air the unused rooms, to turn and air the bedding, and to clean all the windows and shutters. The house seemed to come alive under her touch, to respond to her warmth and enthusiasm, as though it had been sleeping all this time and awaiting only a woman's tender care to awaken it. Matthew was delighted, and Garnet saw that some of the fine lines of worry about his eyes were fading. He looked on contentedly as Garnet played with his son, who would never let her out of his sight.

Garnet sat one evening by candlelight watching Matthew, who was sitting opposite her, across the hearth. He really was quite a handsome man, with his dark, wavy hair, fine brown eyes and gentle smile. Garnet was content. This might not be quite the gay, luxurious life she had envisaged for herself when she left Reginald Baskcomb's house so full of anger and determination, but it was a cosy, contented life. To be appreciated was a welcome, unwonted change.

Garnet began to daydream. Matthew was a handsome man, and relatively successful as a merchant. His shop held a fine display of riding crops and whips and gloves and haberdashery. Moreover, he was a widower. It was not impossible that one day he would wish to remarry. Why should he not choose the woman he evidently appreciated and of whom his little son was fond, too?

It was a not altogether unpleasant daydream. Far from luxury, mayhap, but her gowns would be of decent stuff as a merchant's wife, and sometimes she might have occasion to wear brocade.

Matthew stirred and yawned. "Time for bed," he announced, and rose from his chair. He paused as Garnet stood up and took a candle, then hesitantly he took her hand. "Garnet, I want you to know—how happy I am—Daniel is —that you are here. I thank God for making our paths cross."

Garnet looked into his sombre eyes. He was a sensitive, gentle man. But somehow there was no elation in the thought of marrying him. It was no use. Riches and luxury she had promised herself, and a merchant's wife fell far short of these. She drew her hand away.

"Goodnight, Matthew," she said quietly, and went to her chamber.

One day, satisfied that the house was all in order, Garnet asked Matthew to let her clean the shop. She was on her knees, scrubbing the stone floor, when a young, buxom woman in a dove-grey cloak entered the shop. Matthew had gone back to the kitchen moments before to see to Daniel.

"Good day," said the young woman pleasantly. "Is Master Matthew at home?"

Garnet stood up, soapsuds dripping from her elbows. "One moment, mistress, and I will call him for you," she said, and made to go to the door connecting the shop with the house.

"There is no need," the young woman said, stopping Garnet short by cutting between her and the door. "I shall announce myself."

"Truly, mistress, I can fetch him," Garnet said. "If it is gloves you require, you may inspect what you will in the meantime."

The fair young woman laughed. "I see you are a new servant here," she said, "or you would know me. My name is Mistress Taylor, betrothed to Master Matthew Lambert. I am free to visit him whenever I choose."

She swept through into the house. Garnet, soapsuds staining her gown, stood swaying a little with shock, her daydreams shattered.

FOUR

GARNET sat alone in her chamber that night after giving
Matthew his evening meal. She was ruffled and discontented.
All afternoon she had heard the voices of Matthew and
Mistress Taylor rising and falling in conversation, but
Matthew had made no move to introduce her to his betrothed.
His interest had evidently been fully taken up by his lady
friend, and Garnet forgotten.

She had obviously made too much of Matthew's interest
in her—his kindliness was only the result of his gratitude to
her, that was all. How foolish she had been to think idly of
marriage with him! But he could have told her he was
betrothed. He had made no secret of his love for Sarah, his
young wife, and his sorrow at her death. So why conceal the
fact that he had already spoken for another wife?

Garnet undressed and put on her nightshift. She folded her
clothes neatly and put them away; then her gaze fell on the
little bundle in the corner. It contained nothing now but a
few oddments, including the piece of cloth that had confirmed
her resolve to look for a better life for herself. Garnet untied
the bundle and lifted out the remnant.

Its sheen under the candlelight soothed away Garnet's
irritation. Mistress Susannah could have her Matthew. He
was not the man Garnet sought, the one who could give her
the life she longed for. She must bide her time a little longer,
until an opportunity to better herself should come about. And
that it would come, Garnet did not doubt for an instant. In

39

the meantime, she would continue as she was, ministering to a man who was kind and to Daniel who always looked for her and whose face lit up at the sight of her. She smiled softly to herself at the thought of him.

Matthew left early in the bright sunlight next morning to go to the Exchange on business. Garnet busied herself in the house and Daniel was playing outside, where she could keep an eye on him from the window. Towards mid-morning, Susannah bustled in, elegant in pale blue satin which suited her admirably, Garnet noted with envy.

"Is Master Lambert at home?" Susannah enquired of Garnet coolly.

"I fear he is at the 'Change, but he should be back ere long," Garnet replied.

"Then I shall wait for him," Susannah said, tossing her fair curls. "I shall amuse myself by looking over his haberdashery in the meantime."

"As you wish," said Garnet. She did not like this cool, elegant creature in the least, but, considering it her duty to be polite to her employer's betrothed, she accompanied her into the shop.

"You need not keep me company," Susannah said disdainfully, as if to imply that a servant's company was not at all to her taste. But before Garnet could reply, a piercing cry from outside the shop diverted her attention. The door burst open and Daniel ran in, clutching his arm and wailing. He rushed straight to Garnet and buried his face in her skirts.

Garnet bent over him, murmuring soothing words and rubbing the hurt arm gently. "See, it is not grazed," she said to him. "The hurt will go in a moment."

Susannah let go the gloves she was inspecting and took a step forward. "Come to me, Daniel," she ordered. "I shall be your new mother soon—come to me."

Daniel's tearfilled eyes emerged from Garnet's skirts briefly, to regard Susannah distrustfully and dive back into Garnet's skirts again. Susannah clicked her tongue in annoyance.

40

"Methinks you do it of a purpose," she said to Garnet in a low voice.

"I? Do what?" asked Garnet in surprise.

"You pander to that child—and I know why."

"I do not understand you, mistress."

"Only too well do you understand, mistress," Susannah mimicked. "You pander to the boy so as to curry favour with his father. You know Matthew dotes on him, and you use it to your advantage. Or so you think. But let me tell you, mistress, that it is all in vain. It will not do you the slightest bit of good."

Garnet was thunderstruck at the accusation, and anger began to well up in her throat, but she bit back her angry words before they could spill out. She turned away hastily to hide the reddening flush on her cheeks.

Susannah was tapping her foot impatiently. "I can wait no longer," she said at last, picking up her gloves. "Tell Master Lambert I called on him, but had not all day to waste. Tell him I shall not call again—I shall wait until he calls on me. Good morning."

She swept out, leaving a silent and furious Garnet to rearrange the disordered display of gloves she had left behind her.

That settled it, Garnet decided angrily. If Susannah thought she was playing for Matthew's attention, then the sooner she left this house the better.

Suddenly a thought struck her. If only Matthew were to allow her to serve in the shop with him, then that way she might meet people, perchance someone who would help her improve her lot. Fine goods such as the Italian gloves and ebony-headed riding crops Matthew sold brought many well-to-do folk to his shop, some of them possibly even rich or titled! She would ask him the very next day.

But next day Matthew was withdrawn and silent, and unapproachable. Garnet decided to wait until he was sated with her good cooking in the evening and then she would ask.

41

She busied herself that afternoon baking his favourite apple pasty, and the cinnamon sticks that Daniel loved.

"Daniel like simmon sticks," the little boy said as he crunched them. "Daniel love Darnet." Garnet laughed. Men were all alike, easily pleased if well fed. She gathered the plump, firm little body to her, and felt his sticky fingers cradling her neck. Dear Daniel. Her one regret, if she were to leave here, would be to leave him behind.

Matthew was still silent and thoughtful over supper. As she washed and stacked away the pots and porringers, Garnet put her proposal to him. He thought for a moment.

"Methinks you have enough work to do in the house as it is," he said, "and caring for Daniel too. But if you think it would be a change for you, I would be willing."

"I should love it above all things," said Garnet.

"Then I have no objection," replied Matthew. "I would not for the world have you feel bored or restricted."

And so Garnet came to work in the shop from time to time. She soon learnt from Matthew the prices of the merchandise, and which qualities to extol to the customers, and Matthew laughed to see her delight when she made her first sale.

Susannah came to visit Matthew occasionally, but he always took her into the house and left Garnet in charge of the shop, so she never heard what they talked of. Matthew always seemed quieter and more thoughtful after Mistress Susannah's visits, Garnet noted, and wondered at the effect.

Then one afternoon, when Susannah was in the house with Matthew, Garnet heard her voice high and shrill, audible even from the deserted shop.

"How do I know?" Susannah was crying out. "How many weeks has she been here now?"

Matthew's voice murmured some low reply.

"And in all that time, do you seriously expect me to believe you haven't bedded her? She's a comely enough wench, and you're a normal man, accustomed to the comforts of marriage, are you not?"

42

Garnet stood still, shocked by Susannah's words. They were talking about her! Surely Matthew would deny such a charge strongly? But Susannah's voice was raging on. "You and she, under the same roof and unchaperoned, and you tell me you have not touched her? I don't believe you, Matthew Lambert. Any servant girl would be proud of your attention, and I'm mighty sure that pretty little thing has led you on.

"But I'm not a vengeful woman, as you well know, Matthew. Get rid of her and we'll make no more of it. That's all I ask—get rid of her."

Matthew's voice cut in, low and forceful, and Garnet could hear no more of what was said. Susannah's voice became quieter, as though appeased, and Garnet felt sure that Matthew had agreed to dispense with her services to avert Susannah's wrath.

So that was that, she thought sadly. No need to try to move on of her own accord, for fate had decreed she was to go in any case. It was a pity really, when life had taken on a new and comfortable aspect.

Later, Susannah swept through the shop on her way out. She cast Garnet a disdainful look, tossed her blonde curls and whisked her skirts curiously about her as Matthew opened the door for her.

"Good morning, Matthew, and remember what I said." She was gone. Matthew closed the door and leaned against it with a deep sigh. Garnet felt his eyes on her, and turned away.

"Garnet, come here." His voice was low but authoritative. Garnet came to stand before him. Now he was going to tell her she was dismissed. The old familiar feeling of anger and resentment gushed up inside her. It was unfair!

"Yes?"

" 'Tis time you had a holiday, Garnet. You have worked hard since you came to me."

This was his way of putting it, she thought angrily. Too kindly to say I am no longer wanted.

"So go put on your holiday clothes," Matthew went on. "I shall take you to the theatre tonight. Have you been to the theatre before?"

"I—no—I mean, but what about Daniel?" She was too flustered to think clearly. Was he not dismissing her after all, then? Or was he perhaps going to break it gently after the evening's outing?

"Go quickly and prepare," Matthew said briskly. "Becky, next door, will keep an ear to Daniel once he is abed."

Garnet did as she was bid, serving up the supper and then helping Matthew to settle Daniel down for the night. Then she went to dress. The old dark green gown trimmed with the pale green silk was the best she could muster for the outing, but it would have to do.

"I would I could put up my hair, at least," she said to Matthew when she was ready. Without a word, he went through into the shop and returned with a handful of bodkins. Deftly, Garnet piled up her back hair and secured it with the bodkins, then brushed the side hair down into dark lustrous curls on her shoulders. She was quite pleased with the effect, and Matthew smiled.

"Come now, we must make shift to find a hackney quickly or we shall be late," he said, and helped her put on her cloak. Then he handed her a fur muff.

"A small gift," he said laconically, and opened the door for her.

By eight o'clock they were in the King's Theatre, and the buzzing excitement of the atmosphere soon communicated itself to Garnet. In the pits, where she sat on a covered bench next to Matthew, were a noisy throng of people of all walks of life, maids and mistresses, apprentices and merchants, pimps and prostitutes, all dressed in their holiday best and bent on enjoying the occasion. The air was pungent with the smell of oranges. Garnet sat wide-eyed.

"You have not been to the theatre before?" Matthew asked her. "I thought not," he added as she shook her head slowly.

"See, there are the boxes where the gentry sit." He pointed aloft. Garnet saw them, elegant in their plumes and ruffles and jewellery, and envied them.

Suddenly her breath caught in her throat. There was her gallant from the procession—Nicholas—in company with a group of dandies who were jeering and teasing the plump, pretty little orange-seller in their box.

Garnet could not hear what they were saying to the wench, but she was obviously defending herself with spirit, and caught one of the young gallants a glancing blow on his cheek when he slid a saucy hand into her bodice. Nicholas, Garnet noticed, was laughing uproariously at his friend's discomfiture.

Then an actor with a hoarse, bellowing voice came on stage and began to declaim.

"The prologue," whispered Matthew. "The play is about to begin." And, sure enough, as soon as the man walked off into the wings, the curtains swung back, revealing a grey-haired man striding up and down before a cloth painted to represent a forest.

"That's Charles Hart," came Matthew's whisper again, "one of the best actors Tom Killigrew has." Garnet had heard of the fame of Killigrew, the manager of the King's Theatre, whose profligate son was a bosom friend of the King himself. But her attention was riveted by the girl who came on stage next, her full, voluptuous figure clad in tight breeches and a white shirt, and who strutted up and down like a turkey-cock. Her face, partly masked by the thick layer of greasepaint, was strangely familiar.

She spoke her part in a shrill, high-pitched voice, and something in the timbre of the voice stirred Garnet's memory. Yes, that was it—the girl outside the inn, the actress who would have scratched her eyes out. Chloe, the man had called her.

She watched the pert, pretty creature pace arrogantly up and down, striking poses and pausing every now and again to glance coquettishly at the audience, and smiling to hear the

45

apprentices' whistles. At the end of the act, and again at the close of the play, she sang a saucy, strident song, and stooped eagerly to retrieve the coins thrown on to the stage for her. When the curtains finally closed and hid her from view, Garnet saw the dandies rush out from their boxes and disappear.

"Where are they going in such a hurry?" she asked Matthew.

"To the tiring-rooms, no doubt, to bait the fish of their fancy," he replied. Garnet noticed that Nicholas had been one of the first to disappear.

"That actress who sang?" she asked.

Matthew laughed abruptly. "She or one of the other women," he said. "Madame Chloe has a large following already, including some men who are prominent in high places. She surely must have a maintainer of standing who keeps her well dressed and in a fine lodging of her own. No doubt Madame is well provided for already, and it would have to be a man with much to offer who could tempt her now."

Garnet enquired no further. It was evident that to be an actress was to be in a position to attract attention, and if the actress should happen to possess a fair face and lovely figure as well, then nothing was beyond her reach. Not carriages, nor jewels, nor even rose brocade. . . .

Garnet was silent during the ride back to Cheveril Street. There was much to think about. Madame Chloe had seemed to have little talent beyond being able to sing and flirt. Garnet, too, could sing and dance, and her face and figure were passable—was it conceivable she might be taken on at a theatre when Matthew told her she was to leave?

She looked across at Matthew. He, too, was silent as the coach rumbled and jerked through the dark streets. Was he wondering how to phrase her dismissal? Poor Matthew, he was naturally so sensitive, it would hurt him to have to tell her.

Matthew looked up and saw her watching him. He smiled. "Did you enjoy the play, Garnet?"

"Indeed, yes. It was an exciting new experience for me."

He was thoughtful for a moment. The coach came to a halt at the shop door, and Matthew helped Garnet to alight, then paid the coachman. At the doorway he said, "Garnet, there is something I wish to discuss with you."

So now it was coming. Garnet looked at his earnest face, pale in the moonlight, and could not bear the thought of his distress.

"Not tonight, Matthew. I am tired. Let us talk in the morning," she said gently, and walked ahead of him into the house. "Thank you so much for the muff, and for a delightful evening,' and, taking up a candle, she left him in the parlour and went up to bed.

Matthew watched the slim, cloaked figure with the candle-light gleaming on her glossy black hair disappearing through the doorway. Damnation! What was he to do about her?

He sat listlessly in the chair by the dead ashes in the hearth. What an infernal situation to be in! Susannah, hitherto always so amiable, suddenly suspecting him of seducing Garnet and trying to force him to dismiss her, and all the time he had a sneaking suspicion himself that he was growing too fond of the girl to part with her. And Daniel adored her, there was no doubt of that. He would be heartbroken if she went away.

If only Susannah had not interfered! Everything was fine until she was seized with this stupid womanly suspicion—or was it jealousy? She had been positively sullen and angry this afternoon, but it was not as though she loved him herself. She and he both knew their forthcoming marriage was but a marriage of convenience, arranged by Matthew and her father to further their mutual business interests. And as her father, a big, bluff, hearty Yorkshireman, had said, quite bluntly, Matthew needed a housekeeper and a mother for his son, and

47

Susannah, at twenty-four, was already an old maid, destined to lead apes in hell, as the gossips said, if Matthew did not take her on. It was merely convenient for all parties concerned that they should marry, so why was Susannah acting like a jealous mistress?

It didn't make sense. And now that he was growing to appreciate Garnet and her love for Daniel, it was all going to have to end if he was to soothe Susannah's sulks. It just didn't make sense. But he was not going to be dominated by Susannah. If Garnet was willing to stay on here, then he would prefer to break the betrothal to Susannah if necessary, and be damned to the loss his business might incur. Only Garnet had not given him chance to ask her, as he had intended. It would have to be tomorrow! He was not prepared to lose her just because of Susannah's stupid suspicion.

No, thought Matthew, as he rose from his chair and lit another candle. I won't let her go so easily. He locked the doors and cast a final look around to see that all was well, then closed the parlour door firmly behind him. His mind was made up. He would talk to Garnet tomorrow, as soon as he returned from the Exchange.

FIVE

NICHOLAS stirred and rolled over in his tester bed. Lord! How his head throbbed still! He opened his eyes slowly and blinked at the light filtering in through the casement windows.

He put one foot gingerly out of bed and groaned. What a filthy headache! He shook his head to clear it, then stood up slowly and padded across the parquet floor to the window. A few lungfuls of air, and he began to feel better.

It was his own fault, drowning his disappointment over that actress filly in downing the best part of a butt of Canary wine. He knew he would suffer for it in the morning, but it had seemed better at the time than provoking a fight with Hugo over the girl.

He opened his mouth to shout for Jethro, the manservant, but deemed it unwise to shout in case it made his head ache again. Instead he began to dress, slowly and laboriously. A splash of water on his face from the jug on the washstand made him feel rather more human, and he began to think over the events of the night before.

The visit of the Wreckers to the theatre had been a dismal failure, he reflected. Not one of the fellows had really enjoyed it—no fun, no riot, and none of them had succeeded in getting a decent wench for the night. Except Hugo, of course, but, then, he was in a privileged position.

His lip curled as he thought of Hugo. He was an unpleasant little man, with thick, rubbery lips and a pronounced hump on his left shoulder. But he was a clerk to the Secretary of State at Whitehall, and was in a position to be able to pull strings at Court—a word in the right ear at the right time, and events could take an unexpected course when Hugo was behind the scenes. None of the Wreckers cared for him, but feared him rather, and none had dared to refuse him when he had applied for membership of the Club.

Moreover, Nicholas suspected, they each had a sneaking hope that Hugo might be able to further their own designs. He himself hoped that one day Hugo could be prevailed upon to find him some position at Court which would bring him power and prestige. It wasn't the money. Nicholas was wealthy enough—but Nicholas' family had never done aught to further the Royalist cause and consequently were overlooked when His Majesty had returned to the throne.

In the meantime, all he could do was to tolerate the ugly little bastard and try to keep on the right side of him. That was why he had not called him out over the little actress filly last night. She was a shapely little wench, provocative and full of promise, but she had smiled invitingly on Hugo when she discovered who he was, and Nicholas had been put resentfully out of the running. Pity, too, when he'd been making such good headway with her up till then. Never mind, there was always the chance that Hugo would tire of her soon.

He ran his tongue over his hot, dry lips. God, he was parched! Well, he was due to meet one of the younger sons of a noble family at the Cock Inn in half an hour—he could slake his thirst to the full there. He wondered idly what this young Josiah, so anxious to join the Wreckers' Club, would be like.

Half an hour later he was sprawled on a high oaken settle in the Cock. Opposite him sat a pale, eager-faced youth of no more than seventeen. Between them on the table lay an overflowing flagon and two pewter tankards.

"You know of the activities of the Wreckers, of course?" Nicholas said as he learned forward and filled the two tankards from the flagon.

"Oh, indeed, yes," replied the youth. "It sounds to be just

what I am seeking. Life is so dull, so boring. My father has no time for me, only for my older brother, and I am left with nothing to do but fill my time as best I may."

"I see," murmured Nicholas. He eyed the boy thoughtfully. He didn't look to be very promising material for the Club, but one could never tell by appearances. Take Robert, for example; he was a pale, aesthetic-looking youth who looked more like a monk than a reprobate, and yet he had been one of the Club's most active members, the arch-instigator behind most of their riotous activities during the past twelvemonth. It had been his idea to set fire to the workman's thatched cottage—indeed, it was his hand that kindled the fire after he had removed the water-wagon to a remote distance and barricaded the door. It had been a hilarious sight, to see the old man and his wife choking with smoke, coughing and clawing at the barricade to get out. No, appearances could be deceptive.

"You know, then," Nicholas went on, "that in order to be initiated into the Club you must perform some act of destruction, as the name of the Club implies. It must be done on your own, representatives of the Club being present either at the act itself or soon after to see the consequences?"

"So I understand from Hugo," the boy replied. So it was Hugo who was proposing him for membership, was it? In that case, Nicholas decided, it would be best not to refuse the youth.

The boy leaned forward eagerly. "What kind of destruction must it be? I have already knocked over a watchman's box and trampled it to splinters. Would that suffice?"

Nicholas refilled his tankard; the boy's was as yet still half full. "It must be something of a higher order than a watchman's box, Josiah. Something which was whole and orderly before your attentions. Wreck a house or a tavern, break up some meeting such as a church congregation, destroy something of value, a human relationship, a girl's virginity, or what you will. You suggest and we approve if we deem fit."

51

The boy's eyes flickered. "I could rape a maid," he said. "I am not unversed in men's ways, you know. I have already taken my mother's chambermaid," he announced triumphantly. Nicholas smiled to himself. The chambermaid was hardly likely to be a virgin, he thought; more likely she was the pacesetter in the affair and Josiah the victim.

"As you will," he said quietly. "The rape of a virgin—a virgin, mind you—is an acceptable initiation. But we must have proof."

"That you shall," the lad replied boastfully. "You may be spectators, if you will." Nicholas laughed. Indeed, it might prove an interesting evening, to watch the clumsy fellow's fumbling attempts, but he had better consult with Hugo first.

He called for more ale, and the bushy-browed landlord sent a rosy-cheeked girl to their table with another overflowing tankard of ale. Josiah, as though he thought it was expected of him after the recent conversation, pinched her ample rump, and the girl shrieked.

Nicholas quaffed his ale swiftly, relishing the feel of its coolness on his hot, dry throat. He would leave the young fool to his antics and get home for a meal. Before he left, however, he told Josiah of the Club's next meeting.

"Thursday we meet at Hugo's country place—you know it?" The youth nodded. "Be there, if you can prove your ability to become a member. If not, wait until we inform you of the next meeting."

"I shall be there," Josiah said confidently.

"You have yet to find your virgin," Nicholas reminded him.

"I know of one. And I shall make the opportunity of finding her alone, or, if all else fails, I shall bring her with me to Hugo's, by force if necessary."

"As you will. Till Thursday, then," said Nicholas. He strode out of the inn and took his horse from the ostler. He was glad to be rid of Josiah's company. Youth could be very trying, with its cocksureness and supreme self-confidence. He

52

wished he could be as sure of a pretty maid for himself on Thursday as Josiah was. Hugo always took the pick of the bunch, blast him!

As he rode at a canter down Cheveril Street, he reined in to allow a coach to pass. He did not want to be spattered with mud from its wheels. He smiled and doffed his plumed hat as he recognised the occupant, Lady Caroline. Not that he knew her well, but she was acquainted with his family and she held an honourable position at Court as a Lady of the Queen's Bedchamber, and it was always well to keep in with such as she.

Lady Caroline gave him a cool nod in reply, and her coach drew up outside a shop. By the time Nicholas passed the shop she had disappeared into its dark interior. He hurried home. He was beginning to feel hungry now.

Garnet sat in the shop, the sewing on her lap momentarily forgotten. She had brought the nearly completed nightshirt for Daniel into the shop with her because customers were few that morning, but she did not want to idle her time away. Matthew was still at the 'Change, and Daniel was next door with Becky.

She leapt to her feet as a finely-dressed woman, obviously of breeding and rank, swept into the shop. Garnet laid her sewing aside on the counter.

"I wish to inspect some gloves," the lady said, "preferably some Italian scented ones."

Garnet's heart sank. Of all the fine display of gloves Matthew had, there were no scented ones among them.

"I have some beautifully embroidered Italian ones," she said, hastening to fetch them.

"But not scented?" the lady said.

"No, but one is free to scent them with the perfume of one's choice," Garnet pointed out.

The lady fingered the gloves thoughtfully. "Are you likely

53

to procure some scented ones?" she asked. "I have a fancy to them. All the ladies at Court seem to have them but me."

At Court? Garnet looked up with eager interest. This lady was actually at the Royal Court of His Majesty! "I am sure Master Lambert will do his utmost to obtain some for you, my lady," she said. "I know he expects a new delivery from Italy soon."

"Then tell him to inform me of their arrival, child. Lady Caroline Rosewarne, at Whitehall."

Lady Caroline turned to go, but her gaze fell on the night-shirt lying on the counter. "That is a very pretty shirt," she said, pointing to it. Garnet picked it up. The older woman took it from her fingers. "This is fine stitchery," she commented. "Is this your own work?"

"Indeed, ma'am. I was an apprentice dressmaker."

Lady Caroline inspected the ruffles closely. "It is very fine work indeed, child. I would I had such a craftswoman to do my sewing for me. If ever you should seek another position, take care you let me know, for I could make good use of you."

Garnet's eyes grew wide with surprise and delight. It was too good to be true! Here was she, on the verge of dismissal from Matthew's household and contemplating going on the stage for a living, when suddenly out of the blue she was being offered the very thing she sought most! A life of ease and comparative luxury at Court! She looked at my lady's beautiful taffeta gown. No doubt her ladyship was in the habit of handing on her cast-off gowns to her maids, as was the custom. Now it would no longer be beyond credibility that Garnet could soon possess a brocade gown of her own!

She did not hesitate. "My lady is most gracious," she said, dropping a curtsey. "As it chances, I shall be seeking another position, and I should be most honoured to sew for a lady such as you."

"Then it is settled," said Lady Caroline with satisfaction.

"Arrange it with your master, and come to me at Whitehall as soon as you are ready."

She paused at the doorway. "And do not forget to tell your master of the gloves. Italian, and scented, if you please."

"I shall remember," said Garnet, her heart bounding with excitement and anticipation. She clutched the nightshirt joyfully to her. She looked at its tiny embroidered petals and the ruffles which had brought her such fortune, the ruffles she had lovingly wrought for Daniel. Dear Daniel. I shall miss you, she thought, but it was only a flicker of a shadow to cloud her leaping joy.

She could barely wait for Matthew's return. Finally he came.

"I must talk with you, Garnet," he said.

"I know already," she interrupted him, "but you are not to worry. It is decided."

"What is decided?" he asked, puzzled.

"I know Mistress Taylor wants me out of your house, and I know also that you are reluctant to hurt me. I appreciate that, Matthew, truly I do. But I have been offered another position, and have accepted. I shall leave as soon as possible, so Susannah has no further cause to worry."

Matthew looked thunderstruck. "But I do not wish you to leave, Garnet! Where are you going?"

"To work for Lady Caroline Rosewarne at Whitehall."

Matthew looked down at the floor. "Do you not wish to stay with us, Garnet—with Daniel and me?"

Garnet looked at his crestfallen face. "I shall miss you both, of course, and I shall visit you occasionally, if you will permit me. But I know Susannah will be happier once I'm gone. And, oh, Matthew—this is what I really want."

"I see." Matthew looked up and smiled at her. "Then if it is what you truly desire, Garnet, may God speed you and keep you happy. We shall always be happy to see you again."

So it was settled. Garnet paused at the doorway. "Oh, by the way, Lady Caroline has a strong desire for a pair of scented Italian gloves. I said you would do what you could to obtain some for her."

"Yes, of course."

"And the sooner you get them, Matthew, the sooner I shall be sent back to Cheveril Street to collect them," she said gaily. "So make it soon."

"You can be sure of that," said Matthew gravely.

SIX

NEXT morning Garnet packed her few belongings together
into a bundle. Her fingers were eager and excited as they tied
the knot, but somehow the glow of anticipation seemed to pale
into something akin to regret as she fed and dressed Daniel
for the last time, plumped up the beds and set the house in
order. She must be sure to leave victuals ready for Matthew
and Daniel's evening meal, for she was certain Matthew would
not remember.

Matthew was busying himself in the shop. There were no
customers, but it was as if he wanted to occupy himself there
and not talk to her. Was he, after all, angry; or mayhap
disappointed at her leaving? Did he take it as lack of gratitude
on her part? For he had sheltered and fed her all these weeks
since she had become homeless.

Her heart softened. Dear Matthew. If he was disappointed,
no word of reproach would pass his lips. She cuddled Daniel's
hard, warm little body to her as she murmured goodbye, and
felt his arms tighten about her neck. For a moment tears stung
her eyelids. She put him down quickly, picked up her bundle
and went through to the shop. Matthew looked up.

"Are you ready?"

Garnet nodded. It would be best to get it over with as
quickly as possible. Protracted partings were always miserable.

"I'll call a hackney for you," he said, going to the door.

"Do not trouble yourself," Garnet said hastily. "The day

57

is fine and I shall enjoy the walk. Take good care of yourself, Matthew, and of Daniel. God bless you both."

She crossed to the door, where Matthew still stood with his back towards it. He waited until she reached him, then placed his hands on her shoulders.

"God speed you, Garnet," he said in a low voice. "Please bear in mind that you are always welcome here. This will always be a home for you, if you should need it."

"Thank you."

He stood aside to let her pass. Daniel ran into the shop and across to Garnet, clinging on to her skirts. "Me come, too," he said plaintively. Matthew picked him up.

"Say goodbye to Garnet," he told the little boy.

Garnet turned and hurried out. She could not bear to look at the two pairs of dark, solemn eyes. The cobblestones of the street stabbed her feet through the thin soles of her shoes, but she hastened on, to put as great a distance between her and Cheveril Street as possible.

Matthew prowled listlessly about the gloomy shop. He could not put his mind to anything. Now stop this, he told himself angrily. There is no cause to brood, just because someone you found delightful company has gone away. She meant nothing more to you than that, and, anyway, Susannah will no longer have reason to bicker. Get your mind back on your work, man, or your business will suffer.

He counted the pairs of gloves. He needed a fresh supply. That reminded him—Garnet had said Lady Caroline required Italian ones, scented too. He had better send word to the docks to see if the ship had come to port yet.

Daniel was watching him with his huge, sad eyes. "Darnet tum back soon?" he asked. Matthew sighed. The lad was going to miss her too.

He hoisted the boy up on his shoulder. "How would you like to see the bears?" he asked.

The little boy's face let up. That decided it, Matthew

thought. He might as well shut up shop for the rest of the day and take Daniel down to Bankside to see the bear-baiting. That way they might both forget Garnet for a time.

As Garnet left London and neared Westminster, her misgivings about leaving Matthew and Daniel began to be replaced with excitement again. Whitehall Palace came in sight. It seemed incredible that she was about to knock at a palace door! She found the Holbein Gate and nervously rang the bell. A surly porter let her in, then handed her over to another servant, who led her through a bewildering maze of arched passages and corridors to Lady Caroline's apartments. There he passed her over to a maidservant.

"So you're the new sewing maid my lady warned me to expect," said the fair, buxom girl. "I'm Kate. Come this way, and I'll see you get your bath before you see her ladyship."

She led Garnet through another stretch of seemingly unending passages to a kitchen. There she supervised the filling of a large wooden tub with hot water from cauldrons over the open fireplace, and invited Garnet to undress and step in.

"My lady insists that all new servants are bathed first thing," Kate explained as she scrubbed Garnet's back vigorously till the skin reddened and soapsuds splashed all over the flagstone floor. "She's most particular, is Lady Caroline. Won't have no fleas or lice here. And, as you'll be handling all her fine clothes, she'll be most specially anxious about you."

Garnet marvelled at the ways of the gentry and submitted. There was little else she could do, with Kate so energetic and anxious to please her mistress. Eventually, glowing all over and dressed in a worsted gown Kate brought to her, she was ready to be presented to her new employer.

"Where are my own clothes?" Garnet asked anxiously, seeing no sign of her bundle.

"Have no fear," Kate reassured her. "Your possessions will be restored to you once they have all been aired and fumed."

59

So saying, she led the way along more corridors to a large oak-panelled door. Here she knocked, and in answer to the faint "Come in", she opened the door and led Garnet in.

"The new sewing maid, my lady," she said, and withdrew.

The tall, fair lady seated on a chair at her writing desk turned and surveyed her. "Ah, yes, the little maid from the shop. What is your name, child?"

"Garnet Appleby, my lady." Garnet dropped her a curtsey.

"Turn about that I may see you." Garnet did as she was bid. "Now come here." As Garnet approached her, Lady Caroline took hold of her hands and inspected them. Garnet felt ashamed of their reddened, rough look. That was the result of all the scrubbing and hard work she had put in at Matthew's house.

"These hands are somewhat rough to handle my fine silks," Lady Caroline observed. "I shall call Elise, my maid, to give you some balm to rub on them and soften them. See then that you keep them always soft and supple."

In answer to her ring, the door opened and a slender, dark-haired girl of about Garnet's age entered. She bobbed a curtsey before Lady Caroline.

"Elise, take this girl and give her unguents for her hands. She is to sew for me." Elise curtseyed again and led Garnet to the door. Lady Caroline spoke again as an afterthought. "And, Elise, there is a vacant bed in your chamber, is there not? Let Garnet share the room with you."

The girl stared at Lady Caroline, her face reddening. Then she followed Garnet out.

She paced quickly along the corridor, muttering angrily to herself, now in English, now in French. "A lady's maid share a chamber with a sewing maid! It ees not right! She has no respect for me! *C'est insupportable!* It will be the stables for me next!"

Garnet was hard put to it to keep up with her furiously swishing skirts. Finally, they reached what was obviously Elise's own chamber, a bare little room with a high bed and an unused, unmade truckle bed under the eaves. She slammed the drawers of a chest open and shut until she found a pot of balm, which she slapped into Garnet's hand.

"Here," she said curtly, and swept out.

Garnet smoothed the cream into her hands, then wondered what she ought to do next. She had not been told whether to go back to my lady, or make up her bed, or indeed anything. A search of the chamber revealed no sign of any bedding. Perhaps she had better go back and ask Lady Caroline what was expected of her now.

The corridors of Whitehall Palace were terribly confusing. They stretched on and on, and every turning revealed yet another long sweep of identical corridor. Soon she was abysmally lost.

A door burst open alongside her and a short, hunchbacked man rushed out, his face contorted with anger. "Get out!" a voice behind him cried. "Bring me no more of your slipshod, inaccurate figures, you hear me?" The hunchback closed the door and turned towards Garnet, nearly colliding with her.

"Your pardon, mistress," he said politely, stepping aside to let her pass. His glance alighted on her face, and Garnet saw the angry flush fade. She took her opportunity.

"Would you be so kind as to direct me towards the apartments of Lady Caroline Rosewarne?" she asked. "I am new here, and have lost my way."

"To be sure," he said, his unpleasant face twisting into a smile. "I am only too happy to be of service to a pretty maid. Allow me to escort you," and he took her by the elbow.

Garnet resented the touch of this ugly little man's hand, but did not shake it off. It felt ridiculous to be steered along by a dwarf only as high as her shoulder, but she had no choice. He stopped before the oak-panelled door she remembered. She smiled with relief.

"Thank you, sir."

"Not at all. Perchance you may do me a service in return sometime," said the hunchback, and, with a grotesque twist

61

of his rubbery lips, he turned and was gone. Garnet shuddered, then opened the door.

Lady Caroline soon put Garnet right as to her duties. "And anything else you may wish to know, ask Kate. You will be responsible to her," she finished, and Kate bore Garnet off to the servants' quarters.

"My lady says you are to share quarters with her maid, Elise," she told Garnet.

"I know. Elise is angry with me for it," Garnet said. "I think she considers me beneath her."

Kate chuckled sympathetically. "Elise considers herself above everyone except my lady. Take good care not to cross her if you can help it, or you may regret the day. Mademoiselle Elise has a fiery French temper, and there's many a scullion bears her clawmarks to prove it."

Relieved of her duties early that night, Garnet went to her chamber. As she lit the tallow candle she was glad to find Elise was not yet there, but the truckle bed had been made up and her bundle, now presumably aired and deemed clean, lay upon it.

She opened it and took out her two gowns, then opened the door of the press to hang them away. The press was already full, with everyday gowns of worsted rubbing shoulders with elegant gowns of silk and taffeta. Elise was a fortunate maid indeed, to be so well endowed with clothes. Garnet squeezed her own gowns in alongside the others, then returned to her bundle.

She sat on the bed and picked up the piece of shining red brocade, the talisman by which she had set her life. It had brought her to Court, and—who knew?—she might soon be able to wear gowns like it. Elise's wardrobe showed that she had obviously profited from her situation at Court, and it was possible, even probable, that Garnet would do likewise.

She crossed to the press again, dropping the piece of rose brocade on Elise's bed as she passed. She flung the door of the press open, and fingered the beautiful stuffs of which Elise's

62

gowns were made. Oh, how glorious, how luxurious they felt!

The chamber door opened and Elise entered. Her pale brow furrowed into a frown as she saw Garnet at the press. "What are you doing?" she demanded. "That is my press, and those my gowns." She came swiftly to Garnet's side, and saw the alien gowns in the press.

"*Nom de Dieu!* Get those out of there! How dare you!" she snapped. "I don't want the disgusting rags of a sewing maid next to those of a lady's maid!" She wrenched out the offending gowns and flung them on Garnet's bed. "You will please to take no liberties in my chamber, you understand? You are here on sufferance."

Her gaze alighted on the remnant of brocade on her bed. "You think to take over the whole room to yourself, do you?" she said, swooping on the material and holding it in her fingertips at arm's length. "Please to keep your rubbish away from everything that is mine. Do I make myself clear?"

Garnet hurried to take the brocade. "This, I think, should be burnt," said Elise, jerking it away from her grasp and holding it to the candle flame.

"No, no," cried Garnet. "Give it to me, it is mine! Please give it back to me!"

Elise hesitated. Perhaps the note of pleading in Garnet's voice pleased her and gave her a feeling of power. She lowered her arm. "Very well," she said reluctantly. "You may have it, but you must promise to do as I bid you in future. You promise?"

"Yes, anything," said Garnet rashly, anxious to regain her precious brocade. Elise held it out to her, and Garnet grabbed it eagerly.

Elise undressed for bed thoughtfully. When they both lay in bed and Elise had doused the candle, Garnet heard her voice in the darkness.

"You promised you would do anything, Garnet."

Garnet lay still, wondering what kind of promise Elise was going to extract from her now in return for the brocade. But

Elise said no more. Garnet heard her sigh contentedly and turn over to sleep, and Garnet sighed too. Life at Court was not going to be easy after all, if this creature was going to try to exercise her mastery over her.

SEVEN

Susannah sat opposite Matthew in the parlour. "How long is it now, Matthew—three weeks? And still no word from her? That just shows how grateful she is to you for all your kindness. Forget about her, as she obviously has forgotten you. Let us speak no more of her."

Matthew cleared his throat. "The shoe is on the other foot, Susannah. It is I who shall be eternally grateful to her. But for Garnet, Daniel would . . ."

"Nonsense," Susannah interrupted him. "You make too much of it, Matthew. Too sentimental, that's your trouble. Just because she did what any ordinary person would have done in the circumstances."

A thin wail cut into the air. Matthew rose from his seat. "Daniel is awake. I must bring him down," he said. As he fetched the boy he reflected how sorely he, too, had missed Garnet. Never before had Daniel been one to wail and behave peevishly, but, although he had stopped asking for Garnet, he obviously still felt that something was amiss in his little life. He commented on it to Susannah.

"But he never missed his own mother, so why should he miss her?" she protested.

"He was too young to remember Sarah."

"And he'll soon forget her, too," Susannah retorted.

Matthew sighed. Susannah never seemed to understand, the way Garnet would have done. Despite the sunshine outside, life was dully grey all the time now.

Heavy boots clattered into the shop and the bell rang.

"Excuse me," Matthew said, and left Daniel with Susannah. Perhaps it would be the messenger with the gloves—Matthew had received word from the ship's master that the vessel was in port and already unloading her cargo. The parcel of gloves would be sent up as soon as possible.

A young man with dark, curly hair and merry blue eyes stood, feet astride, in the centre of the shop. He wore sailor's clothes and his face was rugged and weatherbeaten.

"Good day, master. I have a parcel for you," he said.

"Come in," replied Matthew. "Leave it there and come sup a flagon of ale. You must be thirsty."

The young man put down the parcel and followed him without a second bidding into the parlour. Susannah was trying to disengage Daniel's sticky fingers from her skirts.

"Oh—just look at the mess!" she exclaimed, holding her skirt out, then, seeing the stranger, she let it drop.

"This gentleman is from the ship—with the gloves I was expecting," Matthew explained. The youth doffed his cap and stood uncertainly, looking at the floor.

"I see. Then I'll leave you both to your business," said Susannah, and, gathering up her cloak, she made to leave. Matthew went to see her out.

"They are Italian gloves, scented and embroidered," he told her at the door. "Fit for a lady. Shall I put a pair by for you?"

"If you wish," she answered carelessly, and went out.

Matthew shrugged his shoulders and returned to the parlour. The sailor had put his cap aside and was squatting on his haunches, holding Daniel's hands and talking to him. Daniel was amused by the stranger, whose twinkling eyes were on a level with his own, and he was chuckling happily.

Matthew watched the young man with pleasure. Perhaps Susannah was right. Mayhap he took a liking to anyone simply because they got on well with his son.

The stranger straightened up. "A fine boy you have there, master. I'll warrant you're proud of him."

66

"I am," said Matthew, and then they got down to business. Afterwards, they drank ale together and the young man talked of the homeward journey from Italy.

"We began to fear we should never see England again," he said. "What with storms in the Bay, like they were sent by the devil himself, and then this terrible sickness that robbed us of half our crew. Terrible, it was, to see them going down one after the other, like a row of ninepins, and then dying in agony."

"The plague, was it?" asked Matthew, full of concern. He knew how rapidly plague could strike, and how excruciating the pain of death from it could be. Had he not lost his own sweet young wife but two years ago from it?

"No, not the plague, I think, though it was just as swift and terrible. No blains or swellings like the plague. I don't know how this ague is named, but I hope I never see it again," the stranger replied, and, after a few more flagons of ale, he thanked Matthew and was gone to rejoin his family.

Matthew unpacked the parcel of gloves. There were elbow-length lace ones, beautifully embroidered, and silk ones, and all delicately scented with some musklike perfume—just what Lady Caroline had ordered. He would send her a selection from which to choose.

His spirits rose. If he sent word to Whitehall, perchance Garnet would be sent to collect them. He went back to work feeling far more lighthearted.

Garnet was enjoying life. Her duties were not at all arduous, and Kate was kindness itself to her. Elise, however, was cunning and spiteful, and having extracted a promise from Garnet she held her to it, giving her extra work to do which she should have done herself.

"When you've finished hemming that nightgown, you can press it and goffer the lace," she would say, although she knew full well that ironing and goffering were part of her own duties. For the sake of peace, Garnet held her tongue and obeyed. In her spare time, when work was done, she could roam the Palace and explore it, and already she had watched all the visitors in the Stone Gallery and flirted with the liveried menservants. She had even caught a glimpse of His Majesty, virile and handsome and smiling genially in the ballroom as he handed his dark-skinned, solemn little wife down the stairs. A quaint little creature, she was, this Catherine of Braganza, in her old-fashioned gown with the wide, stiffened skirts and her demurely hooped hair, but His Majesty was gallant and charming to her.

Garnet commented on the King's gallantry to Lady Caroline when my lady asked her if she had seen the Queen yet. Lady Caroline sniffed.

"You wouldn't think him so gallant if you saw how Her Majesty weeps sometimes," she muttered angrily, and then bit her lip as if she had said too much. Garnet wondered. There had been many whispered asides in the servants' hall about the King and about his charm which covered his manifold infidelities. Perhaps that was what Lady Caroline meant. She was in a position to know, possibly even a confidante of the Queen. But, whatever they said, Garnet thought His Majesty looked kind and pleasant.

Lady Caroline cut short any further discussion. "I am told the haberdasher has my Italian gloves now," she told Garnet. "This afternoon you may go to Cheveril Street and collect them for me."

So Garnet found herself once more in Cheveril Street. Matthew seemed pleased to see her, although he appeared rather subdued. To her surprise, however, no Daniel came running to greet her. Matthew parcelled up the gloves.

"Where is Daniel?" Garnet asked him.

"Sleeping. He was tired and cross-tempered all morning."

That was unlike Daniel. "And how are you?"

"Well enough, thank you," Matthew answered, quietly. Suddenly he looked up sharply at her. "And you, Garnet? Are you happy at Court? Would you not reconsider and

68

come back to us? Daniel and I both miss you." He looked down quickly, and continued tying the parcel.

Garnet laughed softly. "I am very happy, Matthew. Truly I am. Of course I miss you both, too, and I am grateful to you for your kindness to me when I needed help, but, to be honest, I want more out of life than I had chance of in the old days. More than you could ever give me, Matthew. I'm sorry."

She was sorry to have to say it, but it was true. Matthew did not answer. He finished the parcel and handed it over to her.

"Thank you. Goodbye—and give my love to Daniel," Garnet said, and hurried out before Matthew should say any more.

It was that same evening that Garnet saw again the lady of the procession, the haughty fair lady who had stepped from the coach in Hyde Park wearing the beautiful rose brocade gown. She was gliding along a corridor to the Stone Gallery, a gallant either side of her trying to claim her attention, but the beauty swept coolly on, ignoring their flattery. Kate nudged Garnet as they drew back against the wall.

"That's Lady Frances Stuart, the King's favourite mistress —or, at least, he would wish her to be. But, so far, she's the only one who's succeeded in keeping him out of her bed and keeping his interest at the same time. Or so they say," Kate whispered, eyes shining as she retailed the current gossip. Garnet had heard of Lady Frances, for conversation in the servants' hall was continually enlivened by spicy snippets of gossip about the intrigues of the nobility.

But Garnet had no thought for the King or his amorous pursuits. She had eyes only for the lady. Frances Stuart was wearing a gown of silver brocade this evening, but in Garnet's memory she saw her again in the glorious rose-covered brocade. Garnet walked back to the servants' quarters in a trance. She had done the right thing today, she was now convinced. She had rejected Matthew and a life of merely

69

adequate comfort for one of luxury and wealth. And now she had seen the lady of the rose brocade again, she knew she had chosen aright.

Silently, she reaffirmed her vow never to look back, never to regret, but to fight on until she reached her goal.

Nicholas was frankly bored by the whole evening. The Wreckers were all there as usual, carousing and swearing, spoiling for a fight, but somehow the thrill of the meetings was wearing thin for him. Most of the rich young dandies were considerably younger than himself, and their effeminacy was downright sickening at times.

He had hoped the tedium might give way to something akin to the old pleasure he used to feel, when Josiah arrived, pale and nervous, and clutching by the hand a dumpy, plain wench some couple of years younger than himself. The girl was pale, too, obviously frightened by the noise and coarseness of the Wreckers, and Nicholas could see the droplets of perspiration on her brow which she kept wiping away with a stiff, nervous gesture.

Hugo had been in fine form, apparently well pleased by having Chloe clinging to his arm, though she was head and shoulders taller than he. His smile had disappeared abruptly when he discovered that Josiah, having failed so far in his mission to rape a virgin, had brought his plain, virtuous sister with him, and she was in total ignorance of Josiah's plan.

"You intend to use her?" Hugo had asked Josiah.

"And why not?" Josiah had asked peevishly. "She is a maid."

Nicholas felt a flicker of interest returning, but evidently Hugo's partisan sympathies for Josiah faded instantly. "Get out," he said curtly, "and do not return to the Wreckers until you can prove your qualification to join us." Nicholas could hear the murmurs of disappointment.

So the highlight of the evening had disappeared. For Nicholas no anticipation was left, for once again Hugo had

70

in tow the wench Nicholas fancied for himself. He eyed Chloe covetously. What the devil could such a beautiful girl see in such a misshapen little toad?

Nicholas fumed inwardly, tossing off huge quantities of Hugo's Canary and Malaga to console himself, but he was not too befuddled to take advantage of Hugo's high good humour late that night. Before dawn Nicholas had extracted a promise from him to sponsor Nicholas' introduction to Court the very next evening.

So the whole night was not wasted after all. He had profited to some extent at any rate, Nicholas consoled himself as he watched Hugo return to Chloe's arms. Fuzzy-headed but relatively content, he called for his horse and set off home in the early grey light of dawn.

In Whitehall Palace, Lady Caroline rose early and called for her maid Elise.

"What shall you wear today, my lady?" Elise asked in her high-pitched voice. It was perhaps somewhat shriller than usual, because Elise was angry at being called from her warm bed so early.

Lady Caroline viewed herself critically in the long mirror. She was still wearing her dressing-gown, and her thin grey hair, as yet uncovered by her wig, fell sparsely about her shoulders.

"Something subdued, I think, Elise. Her Majesty is unwell, and it would not be fitting to attend her dressed like a peacock."

Elise listened unconcernedly. Queen Catherine was frequently unwell, and since she showed no sign of being with child yet, her attacks of the vapours could only be attributed to the tight-bodiced gowns she wore.

Lady Caroline snapped her fingers. "I have it—what about the champagne lace? I have not worn it in months!"

Elise sighed. My lady was well aware that her waistline

and that of the champagne lace gown no longer coincided, but she was fond of it and reluctant to admit the difference. Elise fetched it from the closet.

"Is it not a beautiful gown, Elise?" Lady Caroline murmured appreciatively. Indeed it was, and Elise was impatiently awaiting the day when my lady would admit it no longer fitted her and, as was her custom, give it to her maid. She helped Lady Caroline put it over her head, but, much as my lady struggled, the fastenings would not meet. Elise waited hopefully.

"Alas," said Lady Caroline at last. "I am loth to part with it. Do you think, perhaps, the sewing maid could let it out for me?"

"Not again, my lady," Elise replied.

"Nevertheless, let her be sent for, and we shall see," said Lady Caroline with determination.

Elise roused Garnet and bade her make haste to my lady's chamber. "And be sure you tell her the gown cannot be enlarged," she told her sharply. "The last sewing maid let it out for her months ago, and, anyway, she has had it long enough, and she does not want for gowns."

Lady Caroline watched Garnet expectantly as she examined the gown. It was true there was no more to be let out in the seams, Garnet noted. The only possible course was to insert another piece of material.

"Alas, there is no more to be had," said Lady Caroline sadly. "It was a present from France, a single piece of lace, and all of it was used."

"Then I regret there is nothing I can do, my lady," said Garnet. "I am sorry."

"Ah well, *c'est la vie*, as Elise would say," said Lady Caroline philosophically. "I have enjoyed wearing it, but it is done. I have no further use for it now. Dispose of it, Garnet."

Lady Caroline waved her away, then paused as she caught sight of the girl in the mirror. "I have a fancy it would suit your colouring well, child," she said. "Have it for yourself if it pleases you."

Garnet smiled in delight. "Oh, indeed, my lady, it pleases me well. I am grateful."

"Not at all—away with you now and unpick it. And send Elise back to dress my hair presently."

Garnet almost danced back to her chamber, delighted with her unexpected luxury. This was what she had dreamed of, and longed for! A magnificent gown of her very own! Now she, too, would have a fine gown to hang alongside her work-aday clothes, like Elise.

Elise. Garnet's exaltation faltered. Elise was hoping for the gown for herself. How would she take the news? Garnet did not have to wait long to discover.

Elise was waiting impatiently in their little chamber, pacing anxiously up and down. She spun around quickly when Garnet entered, and her dark eyes lit up when she saw the gown over Garnet's arm.

"Well? Can you do aught with it for her?"

"No."

"She has done with it, then? Garnet could hear the greed in Elise's voice.

"Yes."

Elise's smile of anticipation changed to a look of curiosity. "Then why have you it here, if you are not to sew it?" The smile reappeared swiftly. "She has sent it to me!"

It was a statement, not a question, and Garnet hesitated to reply. Elise's hands reached forward to take the beautiful lace from her.

"I'm sorry, Elise. My lady made me a gift of it."

Elise's dark eyes narrowed, and the smile was instantly replaced by a frown. "You jest," she said sharply. "My lady always gives her gowns to me. Give it to me."

Garnet turned away from Elise's outstretched hand.

"Give it to me, I say!" Elise's voice was shrill now.

"No."

Before Garnet could draw breath to say more, Elise's hand had flown up and struck her a stinging blow across the cheek. Garnet's temper rose instantly.

"How dare you strike me! I will not give up the gown!"

"You will do as I say! Who are you, a common slut of a sewing maid, to take what is rightfully mine? Do as I tell you, as you promised, and give it to me!"

Elise fell upon her savagely, and tried to wrest the gown from her. Garnet sidestepped and dealt her an equally forceful blow to her cheek.

"You forced a promise from me which I have kept until now, doing many of your chores for you, but no more. This gown is mine, and I intend to keep it."

Garnet's voice was low but determined, and Elise knew it. She put her fingers to her reddening cheek and began to whimper. "I am superior to you, both in position and in the length of service I have given my lady," she said. "You should not flout my authority."

"You are not superior to me in any way, you little French puffed-up wildcat, and do not forget it," said Garnet firmly. "I am responsible only to Kate and to my lady. I'll have no more nonsense from you; so, if you don't mind," she said, crossing to Elise's press and opening the door, "move your gowns over and make room for mine."

Casting an apprehensive look at Garnet's set and resolute face, Elise did as she was bid.

EIGHT

THERE was no doubt that Garnet had established her supremacy over Elise. When, later that day, Lady Caroline had made her selection from the gloves and bade Elise to return the remainder to the haberdasher, it was Elise who went. Before their fight, Elise would have sent Garnet on such a lowly errand.

So Garnet was left in peace to unpick the lace gown and remake it to fit herself. She sewed every stitch with minute and loving care. The gown was a symbol of her victory, the spoils of war, and she longed for an opportunity to wear it in triumph. She did not have long to wait.

"I shall not need you this evening, Garnet," Lady Caroline told her late that afternoon. "Put on your pretty gown and go down and join the revels. I believe His Majesty is to give a masked ball, and you will enjoy watching."

Garnet was delighted. She stood unobtrusively in an alcove of an antechamber next to the ballroom and watched the lords and ladies, the merchants and their wives, the liveried footmen, all deeply engrossed in cards or conversation. Many of the guests were wearing masks, but Garnet had no difficulty in recognising the King, masked himself and talking to a beautiful woman with dark red hair. She was tall and graceful, the black velvet gown she was wearing a startling foil to the glittering diamonds on her breast and looped in her hair but the intense blue eyes that Garnet could see through the woman's black vizard glittered no less than the diamonds.

75

Garnet saw her take the King's elbow and draw him towards the alcove where Garnet stood. She drew back behind the heavy drapes, and the King and the woman stopped on the other side.

"Really, Barbara," the King's low, resonant voice was protesting. "Sometimes I find your demands overpressing."

"It is little enough to ask," the red-haired woman said with asperity, "after all I have borne for you." She laid the slightest emphasis on the word 'borne' and Garnet was not slow to catch her meaning. So this was the notorious Barbara Palmer, Lady Castlemaine, the King's mistress ever since he had returned to take the throne! This was the woman all London talked of, who had borne children to the King and been able to keep his attention despite his marriage to Catherine of Braganza, and all his other little *amours*. It was rumoured that she and the King both turned a blind eye to each other's frequent paramours, for both were insatiable. But never once had she lost her power over him. Some said she used black magic to bind him in her spell, others said she and His Majesty drank liberally of a love potion secretly concocted for them in the King's laboratory.

But, whatever the reason, it was well known that she held him in thrall. Garnet drew back further against the wall.

"Well?" snapped Barbara peevishly. "I wonder if you would deliberate so long if your precious Frances were to ask you. She can have aught she desires while she keeps you dangling on the end of a string."

"Frances is a sweet, innocent child," Charles replied.

"Innocent? Not she! She's as full of guile as a fox, that one. Mark my words, Charles, she has no intention of surrendering herself to you, no matter what gifts you make her. I know, for she told me so herself."

"And what makes you so anxious to ride in my new calash, may I ask?" the King asked wryly.

The calash, Garnet knew, was the new carriage King Louis of France had sent to King Charles as a gift. She had seen it where it stood on display near the cockpit in Whitehall that same week, where all the courtiers had gone to admire it. And Kate had said the Queen had gone for a drive to Hyde Park in it that morning, accompanied by the Duchess of York.

Barbara hesitated in her reply. "It is a fine coach," she said. "All of glass, and affording a fine view of the occupants to those who watch."

The King laughed. "Vanity, Barbara. You would display your charms for all London to admire, is that it?"

A high, clear voice cut across the King's laughter. "I am glad to see Your Majesty is so happy," it said. Peering through the velvet drapes, Garnet could see the blonde, gleaming hair of Frances Stuart, looped and threaded with silver ribbons to match her silver-braided gown. Her fair beauty was in startling contrast to the rich, vibrant beauty of Barbara Palmer.

"We were talking of the French calash," Charles told her. "It is a mighty pretty coach, is it not?"

"Indeed, Sire, and oddly enough it was of the calash I wished to talk with you," Frances said.

"I have already requested a ride in it on the very first fine day," Barbara cut in sharply.

"How odd!" said the girlish voice. "I was about to do the same."

"I should have thought a game of blind man's buff or hunt the thimble was more to your taste," Barbara retorted acidly.

"Or a romp in the bedchamber for you," Frances came back swiftly.

The King decided to intervene. "I fear lest the coach may come to some harm," he said smoothly. "I think mayhap it were best to wait, at least until the warmer weather comes. It is cold and exposed in the calash, and I would not wish either of the two fairest ladies at Court to catch a chill."

Garnet heard Barbara's hissing, indrawn breath before she burst out, "Sire, as you know, I am in a condition which

77

makes it necessary that I be humoured. I wish to be the first to ride in the calash, after Her Majesty."

Garnet waited anxiously. If it were the King's child Barbara were carrying again, surely he would humour her. He made no answer.

"And if I do not ride in the calash before Mistress Frances does," Barbara went on malevolently, "I swear I shall miscarry instantly."

Garnet understood now. If Barbara's influence over the King was waning now that this fair beauty Frances Stuart had him in her power, she was making use of Charles' well-known love for his children to coerce him. But, before Charles had time to reply, Frances cut in sweetly.

"Oh, la, the whims of pregnant women! But may I also say, Sire, before you decide, that just as surely as milady there will miscarry if she is denied, so do I also swear that if I do not ride in the coach first, I shall never be in her condition."

Garnet gasped. What blatant bartering! Frances Stuart was offering the King her maidenhood at last, in return for this favour! She peered through the curtains again to watch the King's reaction.

Barbara's face was red and sullen. The King stood in amazement, unable to believe his ears. Frances was smiling sweetly and with the innocence of a child, as if unaware of the significance of her words. She flaunted her fan coquettishly before gliding smoothly away.

The King recovered his composure. "Excuse me," he murmured to Barbara, and went to follow Frances.

"Charles!"

Garnet saw Barbara hasten after him. She could not help admiring the cool, calculating manner in which Frances had beaten her rival. She might have the guileless appearance of a child, but there lay a scheming, ruthless brain behind that pretty face. Garnet wondered if she, too, had been downtrodden or put upon in her earlier youth. She was what

78

Garnet aspired to be—ruthless, beautiful, admired and pursued by all the men at Court, and so far not even the King himself had conquered her.

The lady of the rose brocade was all that Garnet could wish for. A group of gallants entered the alcove and began dealing out cards for a game of basset. Garnet turned and saw them concentrating their attention on the cards and tossing cold coins carelessly on the baize, and she could not help thinking that if she, too, played her cards right, she could possibly, one day, aspire to a position of power like Lady Frances.

One of the dandies glanced up from his cards. Garnet felt a tremor of recognition. Where had she seen this tall, fair youth in the lavender velvet before? The young man's keen grey eyes were regarding her with a puzzled look. Evidently he, too, had a vague feeling of recognition, but had not quite placed her.

Then suddenly it came back to her. The sunlight playing dappled shadows on the grass in Hyde Park, the crowd buzzing expectantly as they waited to see the King. It was the young cavalier who had hoisted her up to get a better view of the procession when she first saw Frances Stuart in the rose brocade gown. Nicholas something.

She averted her eyes, remembering how she had eluded him. As she made to move away, he spoke.

"Your pardon, mistress. We did not know there was anyone here. If you are waiting for someone, a rendezvous, perhaps . . .?"

Garnet turned. He looked very handsome with his fine lace cravat and silver sword, and he was smiling with a kind of polite amusement. "Oh, no, sir."

He rose and crossed to her, and his companions, after a desultory glance, returned to scanning their cards. "I have the strangest feeling . . ." he said, and his look was still puzzled.

Garnet realised she was dressed so elegantly he would never

take her for a sewing maid. "Sir, you flatter me, to say I arouse strange feelings in you," she quipped. Would she really pass for a lady, with no jewels or even a fan?

Nicholas took her elbow. "May I fetch you some wine, and perchance I may remember yet?" he said.

"Remember?"

"I swear we have met before. Now where could it have been? At the theatre mayhap?"

"It is possible."

Nicholas's eyes were still clouded and his forehead furrowed. Suddenly he snapped his fingers. "I have it now!" he announced triumphantly. "The Park, the procession! You slipped away like quicksilver—Garnet, you said you were named." The look of puzzlement returned. "But you told me you were but a sewing apprentice. Was it some game you were playing?"

To Garnet's relief, she saw Kate across the chamber beckoning to her. "Excuse me, sir, I must leave," she said, and Nicholas took her elbow again.

"A moment, I pray. Do you live at Court, madame?"

Garnet nodded and hoped he would ask no more questions. It would be pleasant to let him think she was someone of consequence and keep him dancing attention.

"Then I hope we shall meet again soon."

"I am sure we shall. Now I must bid you good even," said Garnet, and hastened to where Kate stood waiting impatiently.

"Come quickly," Kate said. "My lady is wondering where you have been so long."

"Does she require me to sew at this hour?" Garnet asked in surprise.

"No, no. But there was a fortune-teller here tonight, a gipsy girl, and my lady has taken her off to her chambers to foretell her future. When she has done, my lady says she may predict what is in store for us. So make haste, Garnet."

Garnet cast a look back to the alcove. The funny little man had joined Nicholas, and the pair of them were deep in

80

conversation as they went back to join the card-players in the alcove.

So, if he knew the hunchback, it was possible that Nicholas was employed in Whitehall, too. In that event, chances were high that she would meet him again and be able to pursue their mild flirtation. It was a pleasant prospect.

Nicholas reseated himself at the green baize covered table and picked up his cards.

Hugo looked on over his shoulder. Somehow, the cards did not focus, and all Nicholas could see was a pale, lovely face with lively, green eyes that had a mysterious depth to them, and glossy, black hair cascading on to marble shoulders. She had an air of intrigue and mystery that was not in itself unusual at Court, but somehow she was extremely vital and full of allure.

He must have her, whoever she was. He could forgive Chloe for preferring Hugo if he could have this attractive morsel in place of her. What a superb Queen of the Revels she would make for a Wreckers' Club meeting!

"Wake up there, Nicholas, your turn!" one of the fellows protested.

"Ah, yes." Nicholas absently placed more cold coins in the centre of the table. He was still thinking deeply. If he wanted to return to Whitehall, he must be sure to keep in with Hugo. He shuddered as he realised that the unpleasant fellow was leaning close, too close, over his shoulder.

"Poor play for you, Nicholas," Hugo commented in a cracked, rather shrill voice.

"We haven't all your astuteness, I fear," Nicholas quipped, and was pleased to see the creature had swallowed the compliment, for he was smiling his ugly, thick-lipped smile.

"I win, I think," said a dark youth in salmon satin across the table. Nicholas saw Hugo stiffen suddenly, then cross the alcove to where a masked woman in black velvet stood, angrily slapping her fan against her fingers.

81

"Can I be of service to you, my lady Castlemaine?" Hugo asked her meekly, with a flourishing bow. Nicholas and the other dandies rose instantly. To be in the presence of Lady Castlemaine was equivalent to standing in the royal presence. Nicholas saw my lady glance across to them, and she ceased rapping her fan.

She came towards them. The gentlemen all made a leg graciously, and when Nicholas straightened he saw her eyes were still on him.

"Introduce us, Hugo," she said sweetly. "I think we have not met before."

"Sir Nicholas Graveney, my lady."

She inclined her head graciously and gave Nicholas her hand to kiss. "Are you engaged in card-playing, sir?" she asked, indicating the card table with her fan.

"No longer, my lady. We are finished," Nicholas replied.

"Then would you care to pass the evening with a lady in sore need of company?" she asked with a wicked smile. "I am of a mood for distraction this evening."

Nicholas's spirits rose. If anyone was in a position to advance him, it was the King's chief mistress. "With all my heart," he said.

"Then come to my chambers in half an hour," she said, and turned sharply away.

The momentary silence that followed resolved into a murmur of expectation from the men. Hugo smiled placidly. At last the satin-clad youth roared with laughter. "My lady has need of a stout stallion tonight, it seems," he burst out. "His Majesty must have left my lady unfulfilled."

" 'Tis the matter of the French calash," said Hugo quietly. "Frances Stuart has won the day, and my lady Barbara is sorely angered with the King. Do all she asks of you, Nicholas, and your fortune may be made."

Nicholas was content. He pushed the pile of gold coins across the table to the dark youth. "Your winnings," he said with a smile, "but methinks I am the winner tonight."

NINE

GARNET returned to Lady Caroline's drawing-room. Only a few of the candles were burning in their sockets, and Lady Caroline sat back in her velvet-covered chair watching the maids clustered round the hearth.

Shadows thrown by the firelight danced on the wainscoted walls and heavy window drapes. It was only after some moments that Garnet made out the figure of a dark gipsy girl squatting on a stool by the fire, murmuring in a low voice to the maid kneeling before her whose hand she held in hers. The maid's eyes were round with wonder, or maybe alarm at what the gipsy girl was saying, and every now and again she sighed or squealed softly.

"Is it true? Will it really all come to pass as you say?" the maid whispered, gazing up at the dark, solemn face above her.

"You shall see. I am the seventh daughter of a seventh daughter, and I am gifted with a power to foresee. It shall be as I have said."

The maid rose slowly and made way for the next, who knelt expectantly at the gipsy's knees. It was Elise and her face registered scorn and, at the same time, nervousness. She put her hand, palm uppermost, in the gipsy's lap, and then suddenly withdrew it.

"I do not wish to hear," she said, rising to her feet. Lady Caroline's laugh tinkled from out of the shadows. "Afraid, Elise?" she laughed. "I thought you had more courage."

Elise scowled sullenly and pleated her skirt between her

fingers. "Never mind, come help me disrobe and brush my hair for me." Lady Caroline stifled a yawn politely and rose stiffly from her chair. Elise went to her side.

"Who else remains to hear their future foretold?" said Lady Caroline. "Kate and Garnet? The rest of you are dismissed, then. You may go to your beds."

Lady Caroline and Elise went out and the maids moved away, murmuring quietly to each other about the fates the gipsy had revealed to them. The last skirt swished through the door and the door closed softly behind them. Kate and Garnet stood, waiting for the gipsy to speak.

She raised her huge, sorrowful dark eyes to them. "Which of you shall be first?" she asked.

Kate laughed. "My friend here. I am too weary, and all I want is to sit and rest." She lowered her bulk gratefully into a chair on the hearth, opposite the gipsy's stool, and sighed contentedly. "Go on, Garnet. Let us hear what is to become of you. For myself, I prefer to live each day as it comes and not to concern myself with the future. But I should like to know what is in store for you."

Garnet had not taken her eyes from the gipsy's face. She was a handsome girl, slender and weatherbeaten, but with a fine high brow and lustrous eyes. Her nostrils were narrow and her lips sensitive yet firm. Garnet felt strangely arrested by the girl's beauty. She knelt obediently before her and proffered her hand.

The gipsy bent over and took it gently between her own two hands, her black hair falling forward like a curtain so that Garnet could no longer see her expression.

"You are not a lady!" she said suddenly. Garnet realised that the girl was fingering her needle-roughened fingertips.

"No."

"You misled me, in such a fine gown and with such a gracious carriage," the girl muttered. Kate smiled and leaned back and closed her eyes.

"You have led a hard life."

84

Garnet smiled. "It needs no soothsayer to tell me that," she said. "But what of the future? That's what I really want to know."

The gipsy started to croon softly, a strange, lilting melody, and rocked herself slowly back and forth as she did so. She raised her eyes to Garnet's face, and a faraway look came over her. She seemed to Garnet to be in a trance. Behind her, Kate was beginning to breathe deeply and evenly. The coals in the hearth fell and settled, and the room was enveloped in gloom. Garnet began to feel apprehensive.

"Well?" she asked at last.

"The path lies hard before you as in the past," the gipsy said slowly, her gaze reverting to Garnet's hand. "It will not be easy."

"Will I rise from being a maid to—to something better?"

"It is possible. Indeed, the opportunity lies not far away."

"Tell me more!" Garnet's heart beat faster.

The gipsy looked at her solemnly. "There is much trouble for you, soon, very soon. There will be sickness, even the shadow of death."

Garnet's heart lurched. "For me? I shall die soon?"

The gipsy shook her head. "Not you. You will live long, but for someone dear to you. Terrible sickness. Be warned, wear always the unicorn's horn near your heart."

Garnet knew a unicorn's horn was said to be a certain safeguard against the plague, but she was curious as to the identity of the person the gipsy spoke of. Who was there who was dear to her? And she was more anxious still about the opportunity to rise from being a sewing maid. How, and when, she wondered?

The gipsy pushed her hand brusquely away. "I shall tell you no more," she said, compressing her lips.

"Then there is more? Tell me, you must tell me what you see!"

The girl turned her sorrowful eyes to Garnet. "There is more trouble still. I see a man lying dead."

85

"Of the illness you spoke of?"

"No, another. You will be the cause of his death."

Garnet rose in alarm. "I? I could never harm anyone!"

The gipsy shrugged. "Nevertheless, it is written. You will cause his death. I cannot alter what I see, only tell you what will be, and this will happen."

Garnet saw Kate lying back, her eyes wide open in fright. The gipsy rose slowly, picked up her cloak, and crossed to the door, drawing the cloak about her shoulders. She turned to Garnet again.

"It must be," she said again in a low voice. "You will cause the death of the man who desires you, mistress," and she disappeared into the gloom. Garnet heard the door close behind her before she could find her voice.

Her hand trembled as she lit a candle from the dying fire. "Come, Kate," she said as evenly as she could. "Let us dismiss all that nonsense from our minds."

Kate followed her out in silence and went to her own chamber. But Garnet could not dismiss the gipsy's words and she lay awake far into the night, thinking about what she had said.

In the morning Nicholas Graveney surveyed himself critically in the looking-glass in his bedchamber, and was highly pleased with himself. Nothing in the fair-haired reflection, freshly washed and barbered, betrayed the secret he was hugging to himself. That he had lain that night with the King's chief mistress, and had carried himself nobly in her eyes. She had declared herself highly satisfied with his performance, and said she would send for him again ere long.

That was a compliment indeed to his virility. All the world knew of Barbara Palmer's greedy lasciviousness, and for her to have found him worthy of a second visit was flattery indeed. And, what was more, it gave him leave to enter Whitehall. Nicholas had reason to be content. No longer had he need to lean so heavily on Hugo for support to gain entry to the Court. No longer need he bend his will to do as Hugo bad him. No longer need he surrender his doxies to that gruesome creature.

A fair face framed in lustrous black hair floated across his mind. Garnet, the lovely wench he had come across again last night—she would be his, he vowed, and no Hugo would claim her from him.

In Cheveril Street, Matthew was taking down the shop shutters for another day's business to begin. He felt a little uneasy about Daniel, for the boy was reluctant to leave his cot this morning. It was unlike him. Usually he was full of enthusiasm to help his father about the house and shop, but this morning he was strangely sleepy and small-voiced, and his eyes had an unusual brightness.

Matthew set the shop in readiness, saw that the cauldron over the kitchen fire was boiling, and swung it out on the crane before going upstairs again to Daniel. The boy's face was flushed, but that was to be expected in a child just waking from sleep, Matthew reassured himself.

"Would you like some milk posset, Daniel?"

Daniel opened his eyes, shook his head slowly, then closed them again and rolled over with a moan. Matthew's heart skipped a beat. The lad was sick, he was sure of it now. He bent over the cot and raised his son up off the pillow, and realised that the boy's skin was dry and hot to the touch.

There was no doubt of it now; he had a fever. Matthew debated what to do, whether to close the shop again or to send for Susannah to help him with Daniel. The second course he rejected at once. He wanted to care for his son himself, and in any event Susannah had made it pretty clear that she had little fondness for children. If only Garnet were here. She loved children, and Daniel would do anything for her.

There was no choice to be made. He would have to close the shop until Daniel was recovered. The boy was deeply

87

asleep again. With a sigh, Matthew straightened up and went downstairs again. If the lad were no better after his sleep, he would send for the physician.

But Daniel was far from better by the afternoon. He was feverish and fretful, and vomited back at once even the milk posset Matthew fed lovingly to him, and Matthew's misgivings began to give way to fear. He sent word to Susannah that Daniel was ill and that he would be glad of her assistance, and waited hopefully. A woman would know better what to do, how to cool the boy's fever and comfort him.

There was a knock at the shop door. Making sure Daniel was sleeping, Matthew hastened downstairs eagerly and flung the door open. It was not Susannah. It was the young boy Matthew had given a shilling to, to carry the message to her.

"Is she coming, boy?"

The lad shook his head. "Mistress Taylor bade me tell you she would send food and delicacies for him, but she would not come herself. She said it was thoughtless of you to ask her to risk the contagion."

Matthew's raised hopes died again. He was bitterly disappointed in Susannah, but wasted no further time on regret. Daniel had tossed aside the bedcovers and was moving restlessly, moaning, his eyes still closed and a cold, damp sweat on his brow.

"Darnet," the child moaned, over and over again, and Matthew knew he was delirious. "Daniel want Darnet," he kept saying, his voice rising to a whine, and he pushed Matthew's reassuring hand away. "Darnet!" he shrieked.

All day long he slept fitfully, feverish and tossing, and every time he awoke he cried pitifully for Garnet. By nightfall Matthew could bear it no longer. He would send word to Whitehall and beg Garnet to come back, if only for a little time, to comfort his son.

Nicholas dressed and perfumed himself with more than usual care that evening and set off for Whitehall with a lighthearted step. He had two chances of furthering his ambition there now. If he stationed himself in a place of public thoroughfare, such as the Stone Gallery, he would be sure to catch my lady Castlemaine's eye, or, alternatively, to catch a glimpse of Garnet. Either way, he would enjoy the encounter, the one possibly leading to advancement and the other to a more fleeting enjoyment. And if he were lucky and played his cards right, he might even succeed in both ambitions.

Garnet surveyed herself in the looking-glass. Lady Caroline had given her the rest of the evening to herself, and once more she had put on her pretty new lace gown and was anticipating the excitement of Court life. Elise came in.

"Aha," she said, looking Garnet over critically, "so you, too, plan to join the gentry. So do I." She crossed to the press with determination, ran her eye over the gowns, and selected a jade green silk one trimmed with lace. Then she rummaged in a drawer of the dressing chest and produced a couple of fans and, having selected one with ivory fins, she replaced the other in the drawer.

"Could I borrow that other fan from you for the evening?" Garnet asked her. In her mind's eye she could see herself coquetting with a gallant, half-hiding her teasing smile behind its feathers. To be able to flaunt a fan would certainly help her plan to entice, if not Nicholas, then some other courtly cavalier who might help to further her ambitions.

"If you wish," Elise replied carelessly. She was busy applying paint and a black patch to her pale cheeks. She placed the patch in several positions and viewed it critically before she was satisfied. Then she unbound her hair and looped it on either side into clusters of ringlets. Garnet watched and learned.

After Elise had swept haughtily from the chamber, Garnet experimented with her pots of lotions and carmine, no doubt also handed down to her from Lady Caroline. She stepped back from the mirror at last, highly pleased with what she saw, and, after a few practice flourishes with the fan, she started downstairs to the Gallery.

It was not long before she spotted Nicholas. He appeared to be scanning the crowd, anxiously looking for someone, and his face lit up into a smile when he saw her.

He threaded his way through the crowd across the chamber and bowed gracefully.

"Fair Garnet, I am in luck," he said. "Shall we find a secluded corner to sit and talk?"

Garnet's fan gave her the courage to reply teasingly, for she knew he did not yet know whether she was indeed a lady or a sewing maid. She lifted her eyebrows at him over the rim of the fan, to make her eyes tilt provocatively, and smiled inwardly at his obvious captivation.

Half an hour passed in delightful flirtation and Garnet was highly content with her success. Nicholas seemed unwilling to offer to fetch her wine or refreshment, for fear some other dandy would claim her in his absence. He found occasion to take her hand, as if absentmindedly, and toy with it. Garnet let it linger in his just long enough not to discourage his advances. He had reached a point where she felt sure he was about to suggest a secret assignation somewhere quieter and more discreet, when Kate appeared, flustered and dishevelled.

"Mistress Garnet, I've been seeking you everywhere. There has been a message for you, from Master Lambert."

Garnet looked at Kate in annoyance. What an ill-timed intrusion, she thought. What could Matthew possibly want? She smiled reassuringly at Nicholas.

"A moment, if you please, sir. What is the message, Kate?"

Kate hung her head on one side awkwardly. "I think it were best I spoke to you privately," she muttered.

Nicholas clicked his tongue in annoyance. Garnet rose and turned to him. "I shall be back directly," she promised.

Outside in the corridor, she rounded on Kate. "Now what is the message, Kate? Surely it could have waited?"

Kate shook her head. "Well, I dunno, I'm sure, what I should have done for the best. The messenger said to tell you Master Lambert's lad is ill, sorely ill, and his father fears the worst. The boy is crying for you in his delirium, and Master Lambert begs you to come as soon as you may."

Garnet's heart missed a beat. Daniel, dear little Daniel, mortally ill? She forgot her momentary irritation and patted Kate's arm. "I shall come. Thank you, Kate. You did what was right."

She must ask Lady Caroline's leave of absence at once, but she was sure my lady would agree. All thoughts of Nicholas forgotten, she made for the staircase. Then suddenly she heard his voice calling her, but she gathered up her skirts and hastened away so as not to be kept from Daniel a moment longer than was necessary. Nicholas could wait.

TEN

LADY CAROLINE could not have been kinder or more understanding. She was still up and reading in the library by candlelight.

"Of course you must go at once, child," she said, "if the boy means so much to you. I know you will return as soon as he is well."

"But of course, my lady."

"Then pack and go as soon as you may. I shall not pay your wages in your absence, mind, so come back directly he recovers. I shall look forward to your return, for I have never before had a maid who sews as finely as you. You are a good worker, Garnet, and if it is the plague, you must take good care not to catch the contagion yourself. A snip of your own hair, they say, cut up finely and drunk in a glass of wine daily, is an excellent prevention."

Smiling and nodding her approval, Lady Caroline waved Garnet away. Back in her own chamber, Garnet changed out of her fine gown into her everyday worsted one, and packed her belongings into the bundle. There was no sign of Elise. Presumably flaunting her finery, she was still enjoying herself downstairs.

Garnet flung on her cloak and hastened down the broad flight of stairs and along the intersecting corridors towards the outer gate. Hurried footsteps pursued her, but she did not pause to look back. The only thought in her mind was to reach poor sick little Daniel and to reassure his distressed father.

At the outer gate a hackney carriage stood under the torch-light awaiting custom. The coachman sat slumped in his seat, taking a nap while he waited. Just as Garnet was about to hail the coachman, the running footsteps behind her rang out more clearly on the cobblestones, and a breathless Nicholas caught her arm.

"So? You would evade me yet again, my beauty?" he said, his smile gleaming in the torchlight. "You play a come-hither game with me, leading me to hope for the fulfilment of all my desires, and then disappear like a will-o'-the-wisp."

"Let me go, Nicholas. My errand is urgent."

"No more urgent than my desires, I am sure of that," Nicholas replied. "Have you some secret assignation with another? Do you want all the gallants in London at your feet?"

"Nicholas, please. It is a serious matter and I can waste no time."

"Then let me ride with you."

Garnet was irritated by his persistence. Minutes ago it had been fun, but now Daniel and Matthew needed her, and flirtation was an irrelevant pastime by comparison. She shook Nicholas's hand off her arm.

"Let me go."

"No, i' faith, I will not let you go to some other fellow," Nicholas retorted peevishly. "You are mine and I'll not let you go. You have no right to tease me so."

Garnet flung his enveloping arms away from her. "How dare you!" she snapped, and as he advanced closer again she swung her bundle up and at his face. As he reeled back under the force of the blow, she cried out to the coachman, "To the haberdasher's, Cheveril Street, as fast as you can!" and clambered unceremoniously into the carriage.

Nicholas recovered his balance and clawed at the carriage door, but Garnet held it tightly shut and the coachman, using his whip to good advantage, drove furiously away from the Palace gates.

Nicholas was indignant. Not only was he spurned by a flighty wench, but humiliated before a coachman, too. Fuming and kicking angrily at pebbles in the courtyard, he went back into Whitehall Palace, vowing he would pay that minx out for her cruel treatment of him, the devil have his soul if he did not.

His anger abated as he entered the ballroom, and across the thronged floor he saw Barbara Palmer, standing alone and watching the scene with sullen disinterest. He threaded his way to her, but as he neared the corner where she stood he saw to his dismay that His Majesty the King had engaged her in conversation. Barbara's eyes flickered angrily as he spoke, and Nicholas drew close enough to hear their conversation.

"I trust Mistress Stuart is not wanting in showing her gratitude to Your Majesty," Barbara was answering the King haughtily. "I gather she had fine weather for her drive in the calash this morning." She wielded her fan dangerously close to the King's face, snapping it back and forth in sharp, angry little movements.

"Come now, Barbara, it is childish of you to indulge in such petty jealousy," he answered her smoothly. "You, too, shall have your turn to ride abroad in it, I promise you."

Barbara raised her eyebrows. "You are mighty anxious to please all of a sudden, Sire."

He smiled, his dark eyes glowing, and spread his hands expressively. "I am always anxious to please you, mistress. As I shall prove, if I may come to your apartments this evening."

Barbara snapped her fan shut. "So that's it. My lady Stuart is not willing to honour her bargain after all. I knew it! I warned you so, but you did not believe me." She smiled in self-satisfaction.

"We shall meet later for supper, then?" the King asked.

Barbara's eyes glinted ominously and Nicholas saw her then

94

look at him over the King's shoulder and smile as she recognised him. "Sire, it pains me deeply to have to disappoint my sovereign," she said sweetly, and swept him a taunting curtsey, "but I fear I have already promised my company this evening to this gentleman here," and, so saying, she held out her hand to Nicholas. In bewilderment Nicholas took it, and Barbara led him triumphantly from the hall.

On the way to Cheveril Street, Garnet sat impatiently hunched forward in her seat, holding her bundle close to her on her lap. Poor Matthew, she thought. He would go out of his mind if aught were to befall Daniel. His son was the light of his life, she knew, since he lost his wife. She willed the rumbling coach to move faster, but its wooden wheels seemed to clatter more slowly and clumsily than usual across London's cobbled streets.

When Matthew opened the door to her his eyes were wide and distracted. He took Garnet's hands in his and murmured, "Thank God you are come, Garnet. He has called for you so much." Then he led the way quickly upstairs to Daniel's little chamber.

He hung anxiously over the cot. Daniel was sleeping, his hair clinging to his brow in damp tendrils, but Garnet was shocked to see how thin and wasted his normally chubby cheeks had become. And the waxy pallor of his skin gave him the appearance of being already in death's grasp.

"Help him, Garnet. I beg of you help him," Matthew muttered hoarsely.

Garnet laid her hand on his sleeve. "I will do what I can, you know that. I shall not leave until he is recovered."

Matthew patted her hand in thanks and nodded silently. Garnet laid her cloak aside over a chair, and felt the baby's brow. He was unbelievably hot and clammy, unnaturally so, Garnet thought. She had little knowledge of tending the sick, but it seemed common sense that she should try to cool the boy's raging heat.

"Have you sent for the physician?" she asked as she cooled the hot little forehead with a rag dipped in cold water from a pewter dish.

Matthew nodded. "Aye, he came yesterday and promised he would return again today."

"What did he bid you do for Daniel?"

"He bled him and bade me keep him warm and covered. No more. No food, he said, for he would surely bring it back."

The bell downstairs rang. Matthew went down to answer, and Garnet felt a cool draught of air in the hot, stuffy little chamber as he opened and closed the door. The heat was overpowering, for even the fire was lit in the grate, the windows closed and the curtains drawn tight. It smelt foetid with the brackish odour of vomit, so Garnet threw back the window coverings and opened the casement a few inches, to air the room a little. Daniel stirred and moaned, and Garnet sat down by his bedside, holding his feverish hand and murmuring soft words of comfort.

The door opened again and Matthew entered, followed by a small, sandy-haired man with spectacles, and a wilting nosegay of herbs in his hand. "Doctor Pringle," Matthew said. Garnet nodded to the man, who stood just within the door and would not approach the cot.

"How is the lad today?" he asked cheerfully enough, craning his head forward, but not moving an inch.

"No better, I fear," replied Matthew.

"Fever? Vomiting still? Delirious?" Doctor Pringle queried briskly, and as Matthew bowed his head in answer to each question, he buried his nose deeper in the bunch of herbs.

"I see. Then continue the treatment as I told you, and do you and your lady there," he nodded towards Garnet, "take special care not to catch the infection yourselves."

"Then you know what he is sick of?" asked Matthew, ignoring his mistake. "Is it the plague?"

The doctor shrugged his shoulders. "Who can say? It may

be, and we shall know if the carbuncles appear, or it could be spotted fever or the quartan. Let it suffice that the treatment is the same and he is unlike to recover whatever it may be." He paid no regard to Matthew's wide-eyed stare of horror. "The chief problem is to safeguard your own health, my dear sir, and I would suggest that you and the lady attempt to clear the foul air in this house.

"Burn on your fires pitch or frankincense, amber or wood of juniper. Or, failing these, brimstone will suffice. Perfume your clothing with aught that is pleasant to the smell, make pomanders of rue and angelica and carry them with you wherever you go."

Garnet felt a cold chill of horror clutch her lungs and refuse to let her breathe. This man had coldbloodedly dismissed the child's life and no longer concerned himself with doing aught to help him. He wanted only to preserve the father, so that his bill might be paid. She felt her anger rising, but for the moment held her tongue. It was Matthew who protested.

"But what of my son?" he cried, and there was agony in his voice. "I will not let him die! What can be done for him? You must do something!"

The doctor spread his hands, then quickly returned the herbs to his nose. "Of what use? I could prescribe a posset of fennel and marigolds to expel the poison, but you tell me he vomits all back. The most one can do is to keep him warm, and encourage him to sweat. Hot bricks soaked in vinegar around him, plenty of blankets." His eye lighted on the open window. "Od's fish!" he snapped. "Do you not know that night air is noisome and will harm even a healthy body? Close the window at once!"

Matthew crossed to the window, closed it and drew the drapes. Doctor Pringle nodded briefly to Garnet and made to go out again, but Matthew stopped him.

"Doctor Pringle, you know I lost my wife despite all your efforts . . ." The doctor murmured something in an embar-

97

rassed undertone. "And I would give my right arm, nay, all I have to keep my boy," Matthew went on quietly. "If there is aught you can do, no matter what the cost, I beg you to save him."

The doctor hesitated, then put down his bag with a sigh. He approached the cot and drew back the covers. Garnet heard him sigh despairingly as he surveyed the tiny, pallid figure that lay inert and barely breathing.

"I could let some more blood," he suggested weakly. "It might draw off more of the evil humour," and he reached into his case for a scalpel. Matthew bowed his head. Garnet froze for a second in horror, then leapt to her feet.

"No, no," she cried, restraining the doctor's hand as it brought the knife down to Daniel's small, thin arm.

"Madam, do you interfere with a doctor's better knowledge?" Dr Pringle protested, his face, pink and pudgy, level with her own.

"You cannot bleed him more!" Garnet cried. "See how drained and white he is already! You cannot take from him the last of his life-blood! I will not let you!"

She caught sight of Matthew's face, gaunt and haggard, over the doctor's shoulder. She let the doctor's arm go. "I am sorry, Matthew. It is none of my business, but I love Daniel too, and I cannot stand by and watch him bled to death."

Matthew took her elbow. "You are right, Garnet. Doctor Pringle, I fear bleeding is not the answer, for Daniel is too weak."

Doctor Pringle straightened his back and dropped the scalpel back into his case. "As you wish," he said drily. "He is your son." He snapped the case shut and went to the door. "I shall not visit you again, Master Lambert. I fear I have exposed myself to the contagion too long as it is. And if this lady feels she knows best how to cure a body doomed to die . . ." He shrugged expressively. "I shall send you my bill in a day or two. Good even to you both." He buried his face deep in his nosegay again and left hurriedly. Garnet looked up into Matthew's dark, haunted eyes.

"I'm sorry, Matthew. I should not have interfered."

Matthew smiled faintly. "You acted as I felt, and I'm glad you did. With your help . . ."

"Of course. Together we'll make Daniel well again. I know we will."

A faint moan came from the cot. Garnet bent over the boy. He opened his eyes, bloodshot and shining with a fierce, unnatural brilliance. His cracked lips parted and Garnet heard him whisper. She bent closer to him.

"It's all right, Daniel, we are here. Would you like a cool drink?"

His lips moved. "Take the hurt away, Darnet," he breathed. Garnet heard Matthew's breath catch in a sob.

"I will," she promised. "Where is the hurt?"

Daniel's hand fluttered feebly to his forehead. Garnet stroked it gently. "Here, my lamb?" Daniel closed his eyes in assent. Garnet straightened up and faced Matthew. She was shaken to see the dark, tear-filled eyes. As she had feared, his son's danger had almost robbed him of all power to reason.

"Matthew, will you let me nurse Daniel as I feel best?"

He took her hands in his. "Do what you will, Garnet."

She drew her hands away. She must be calm and practical at all costs. "Then fetch me a truckle bed that I may sleep here by Daniel. And do you then go and sleep yourself."

Matthew went silently and fetched the bed and blankets. In the meantime Garnet bathed the boy's head and hands and fevered limbs with cool water, then moistened his parched lips and removed several of the blankets from the cot, and finally opened the casement window again, carefully screening the cot from any draught. Matthew stood by expectantly.

"He is sleeping peacefully now," Garnet said at last. "There is no need for us both to watch over him, and as you have lost much sleep already, do you go to bed now and I'll stay here." Seeing Matthew was about to refuse, she went on,

"Have no fear, I shall wake you if there is aught to tell you. Go you now and rest."

She ushered Matthew towards the door. He stopped and turned. "God bless you, Garnet. What should we do without you?"

She smiled. "Good night, Matthew. Sleep easy."

There was a faint drift of a smile on his haggard face as he closed the door. Garnet sighed and sat down on the truckle bed, not bothering to undress. She drew her bundle to her, and untied it. Her other working gown lay inside, the fine lace one and a few oddments. But no rose brocade. It was odd, but Garnet did not feel the rise of alarm and dismay she might have expected at losing her treasured piece of brocade. Where could it be? Not that it was important . . . Suddenly she realised that Elise must have stolen it in spite, knowing how she treeasured it.

Garnet laughed inwardly, uncaring. Yesterday it would have been a terrible blow, but tonight its importance seemed to have paled into insignificance compared to the reality and terrifying possibility of Daniel's death. She pushed the bundle aside and crossed to look at him again. He was breathing quickly and in shallow little breaths, but he seemed cooler than before. She lay down on the truckle bed, and determined to keep awake at all costs.

Towards dawn her eyes were sore and heavy and it was a great temptation to let her lids drop, but when she heard Daniel move and groan she leapt to her feet instantly. Before she reached him he had vomited bile and was lying awake and wide-eyed. Garnet's heart lurched when she saw there was blood in the bile.

Outwardly calm and assuring, she mopped the boy clean and changed his sheets and nightgown carefully. She must remove all traces lest Matthew should be horrified.

Matthew came in just as dawn was breaking. He leant anxiously over the cot. "How fare you now, my boy?" he asked, seeing Daniel was awake. Daniel smiled weakly.

"He has slept well," Garnet reassured him.

"And you, too?" Matthew asked, his own eyes red and deep in their sockets, showing he had slept but little.

"Put the cauldron on the crane to boil, and let down the shutters," Garnet said briskly. "There is much to be done."

"The shutters?" Matthew repeated in surprise. "I have not opened the shop since Daniel was taken ill."

"But now I am here to care for him, and you are free to do your business," Garnet pointed out. "However, it will give you less time to brood and worry. Come now, some hot water, if you please. I think mayhap Daniel will take a little posset today."

She followed Matthew down to the kitchen and busied herself in preparing a drink of small beer with warm water and caraway seed. "You know, Matthew," she said casually as she stirred, "I think mayhap it were best if only I were to enter Daniel's chamber, to make less chance of catching the infection." Though her words were casual, the thought had been carefully prepared. There was no sense in risking Matthew's life as well as her own. Suppose Daniel were to survive, only to lose his father? Where would be the sense in that?

She did not look at Matthew's face because she knew how hurt he would be to be excluded from his sick son's chamber. To her surprise, he did not answer. She looked up from the pewter bowl in her hands. Matthew was standing by the fireplace, one foot on a dogiron, gazing thoughtfully into the fire.

"If you wish it," he said quietly. "You are the physician now, and I agreed to let you do as you thought best."

He went quickly away into the shop. For all his apparent agreement, Garnet knew he was sick at heart to be separated from his son. But he had faith in her, and Garnet vowed inwardly that she would do all in her power to justify that faith.

In the afternoon a note came from Susannah, and a little parcel. Matthew read the note and then tossed it on the table.

Clicking his tongue impatiently, he returned to his customer in the shop. Garnet picked up the note.

"To protect yourself, steep some juniper or bayleaves in vinegar, and breathe the fumes frequently," it said. "It is also said that to smoke is a good protection, so I would suggest that you begin to smoke a pipe.

"I send you also an amulet, which I bought for two shillings from a gipsy, and she swears to its efficacy. Wear it about your neck. Yours in friendship, Susannah."

Garnet put the note down. It was no wonder Matthew was angry. Susannah had made no mention of Daniel or enquired how he fared. She cared only for Matthew's welfare and naught for the child. Garnet suspected that Susannah's parcel, containing the gipsy's amulet, would remain unopened.

It did.

ELEVEN

FOR the next three days and nights Garnet never left Daniel's side except to prepare possets for him and to launder his frequently soiled bedlinen. Again and again he spewed up even the brew of herbs and water she fed to him, but at least she was glad to note that there was no blood thrown up on his sheets. From time to time he suddenly terrified her by jerking into a stiff, cramped posture, lying rigid and staring at her with a hideous squint, then gradually relaxing until his eyes readjusted themselves.

It was painful to have to refuse Matthew, who came often to the door to ask how Daniel fared, and to beg a glimpse of him.

"See to your shop, Matthew," she said firmly each time he asked. It was not only to keep him from infection, but also to spare him the harrowing sight of his beloved boy, faded to only a spectre of his normal self. To see the poor child heaving and retching, with barely even the strength to draw another breath, and hear him cry piteously for relief from his pain, would have wrenched sobs from even the stoutest of men.

By night, Garnet lay on the truckle bed next to Daniel, but never once did she let her eyes close in case he called for her. By the third day her eyes felt stiff and her lids scratched against her eyeballs, but she was determined not to sleep till Daniel was on the mend.

But Daniel showed no sign of improving. He grew visibly thinner until his skin was taut across his bones, his eyes sunken and dulled, and nothing would remain in his stomach for more than a few seconds. He lay silent in a coma. Garnet felt despair begin to creep over her, and rejected it instantly.

She threw on her cloak. "I am going to the apothecary," she told a startled Matthew as she darted from the house. She remembered having seen an apothecary's sign not far away, and she sped thither as past as she could. Rain drizzled persistently against her face, and she did not pause to pull up her hood.

Up a flight of stone stairs she found the apothecary's shop. Jars and bottles of coloured liquids and a stuffed crocodile did not hold her interest—her errand was too urgent.

"A child lies dying," she told the wizened little man in faded black. "I must have a cure, no matter what the cost."

"Hold hard, mistress. I can distil no magic potion without knowledge of the ailment it is to cure," the little man protested, waving his hands at Garnet's pressing urgency. "Tell me first the signs," and with many questions as to Daniel's symptoms, he finally nodded and crossed to his bench.

"Saffron first, for the poison in his body," he murmured as if to himself, and reaching for a jar. "Purslane and fennel for the fever to make him sweat, and nightshade to cure the headache. And let me see . . ." He glanced up at Garnet and ran a critical look over her. "Unicorn's horn is very dear," he said, as if to imply she could not afford it.

"How much?" Garnet counted the coins in her pocket.

"Not enough. But no matter, mithridate or bezoar will do as well. Bezoar stone, I think," he added pensively, stroking his grizzled chin with a thoughtful finger, then fetched out some grey, stonelike material from a cupboard.

He pounded and pulvered, mixed and stirred. Garnet saw him take jars labelled hartshorn, sorrel, ambergris, wormwood and valerian among others, but which he used she knew not.

"Only make haste," she begged. "The child is mortally sick."

At last the apothecary handed over a repulsive-smelling

decoction. "That is fresh cow dung," he said, noting Garnet's expression, "but you may disguise it by giving the child a spoonful of this in wine or rosewater."

Garnet paid him and hastened back through the rain-soaked streets, paying no heed to the fact that her thin-soled shoes were drenched and squelching. She forced a spoonful of the revolting mixture between Daniel's unresisting lips as he lay unconscious, and tried to wash it down with water. Some of it spilled out of the corners of his lips.

Two hours later she tried again, with a little more success. He was still quite unconscious. Then she lay down on the truckle bed to rest. All night she lay awake beside the silent figure, and more than once she heard Matthew's footsteps come quietly to the door, pause, and then fade away again. She watched the first streaks of dawn creeping across the London skyline, and then suddenly Daniel stirred. She rose and crossed to him at once.

"Daniel hungry," he murmured weakly. "Daniel hungry."

Garnet's heart leapt in joy. He was going to recover! The vile decoction must have worked after all! She bent over him and smoothed the tangled black curls from his brow.

"I will fetch you food this moment, my precious, just you wait patiently," she murmured, then sped down to the kitchen. While the milk warmed over the fire, she fetched out the posset-pot and carefully mixed a caudle of white wine and warm milk with sugar and cinnamon. As she ladled the mixture into the posset-pot, Matthew appeared, blinking his red eyes. A smile flickered across his face.

"My poor lass, you look worn out," he said quietly. "It is time you slept. Let me tend Daniel today. I can leave the shop shuttered and you can sleep undisturbed."

Garnet turned to him, her fatigue gone. "Matthew, he is on the mend, I know it! He is hungry. It is a good sign, and I know he will grow strong again now."

A light crept into Matthew's haggard eyes. "If he recovers, and I pray God you are right, it will be all your doing,

105

Garnet. But go you now and sleep. I will take him the posset."

Garnet brushed his hand aside. "I will finish the job I have begun. 'Twould be foolish to expose you to infection now." Seeing his saddened look, she added gently, "But tomorrow, if he continues to improve, you shall tend him, I promise."

She hastened back to Daniel's chamber with the posset. This time he took it greedily, and smiled wanly when it was done. Garnet waited, but he brought none of it back. She breathed a sigh of relief. Gently, then, she bathed and changed him, and winced to see the ribs and collarbones that almost protruded through the lad's tight skin. Never mind, she thought defiantly, careful nursing and plenty of good food would soon build him up again.

In the succeeding days the unearthly pallor and dark circles began to fade from Daniel's face. Garnet cooked him wholesome broths of chicken and vegetables, and the hollow cheeks began to fill out again. Matthew wept openly over his son's cot, holding the little body close to his chest, but whether his tears were of relief and gratitude, or of dismay at seeing what his son had shrunken to, Garnet did not know.

Matthew came into the kitchen one day, followed by Doctor Pringle.

"Will you have a tankard of ale, Doctor, or some wine?" Matthew asked him.

"Thank you, no, Master Lambert. I have called only about my bill. I must say," the sandy-haired doctor said, glancing about him, "I expected to see the house draped in black and the mirrors turned to the wall. Do I take it, then, that the lad is lingering on yet?" There was an air of genuine surprise on his face. Obviously he thought Daniel dead days ago.

"He not only lives, he is recovering," said Matthew quietly but proudly. "Thanks to the ministrations of Mistress Garnet here." He took her arm. "Twice now she has saved my son's life. Twice over I owe her all I possess."

The doctor blinked unbelievingly at her. "You amaze me," he murmured. "He had all the signs of death on him already."

106

"But Garnet was reluctant to let him go. She has more courage and determination than one would think in that small frame," Matthew said softly, and Garnet could hear the grateful affection in his voice.

"I must go. My patient is thirsty," she laughed, and took Daniel his drink made from conserve of red roses, leaving Matthew to settle his business with the doctor privately.

When at last Garnet allowed Matthew to persuade her to rest, she slept long and deeply. She surveyed herself in the mirror the following day and was horrified to see the gaunt look and crepe-like circles about her eyes. But what of that? Daniel was alive and well on the road to recovery at last, despite the doctor's prognostications. Sleep would soon restore her temporary loss of looks.

She looked about the house. Everywhere was filthy and untidy, neglected since Daniel fell ill. She set to now, to scour all the dishes with bran and soap, and to scrub the floors and the deal kitchen table. Then she laundered all the sheets and towels and polished the furniture with beeswax, while Matthew played with Daniel and amused him. And Daniel was ecstatic to have his father's undivided attention all to himself. The sparkle came back to his dark eyes, and his baby cheeks filled out and grew rosy again. Garnet was content and had a cosy feeling of satisfaction at the results of her handiwork.

Time passed. Daniel was at last recovered and out of his cot, playing contentedly downstairs again. Matthew reopened the shop. Susannah sent word that she would come to visit shortly, once Matthew was positive that all contagion was gone. Matthew sniffed and made no comment on her message.

Life was more less back to normal in Cheveril Street and Garnet began to feel restless. She had sent no message to Lady Caroline since leaving Whitehall, and knew that my lady trusted her to return as soon as possible. Garnet felt her work here was done, and it was time she returned. And, more than that, she was beginning to miss the excitement and intrigue of

Court life. She had had no time to regret it while Daniel was so desperately ill, but now . . .

Nicholas was furious and his pride was hurt. Lady Barbara had professed herself very pleased with his deportment and had welcomed him to her chambers open-armed for over a week, and then suddenly she scorned to recognise him even in the public rooms at Whitehall. It was well known that she was flighty, but to use him and then discard him so abruptly, without even an excuse, was unforgivable.

To make matters worse, he had boasted loudly to all the Wreckers of his latest and most impressive conquest, and they had listened in breathless reverence to the man who had supplanted the King himself in milady's bed.

"What is she playing at?" Nicholas asked Hugo irritably one afternoon as they sat supping ale in the parlour of Hugo's lodgings. Hugo kept lodgings as well as his apartments at Whitehall, for the better convenience of keeping his affairs discreet. Hence Whitehall never came to hear of his mistresses or his Wreckers' Club activities.

"I thought you said pleasing her could lead to advancement for me," Nicholas grumbled.

Hugo shrugged his misshapen shoulders. "Who can say? I said it could, not that it would. Women are ever unpredictable, my friend, as you should know. But I do know she has changed her policy where His Majesty is concerned."

"You mean she no longer needs to use me to spite him?"

"I know she refused to acknowledge milady Frances any more after *la belle* Stuart won the battle of the calash. She would not admit the Stuart to her apartments for supper again, and the King refused to go unless she was allowed to come with him. Milady Palmer changed instantly. Now she clamours for milady Frances' attention, claiming to be her closest friend. They even sleep together now, so inseparable they have become, so that is probably why you were banished from her bed."

Nicholas growled and kicked peevishly at Hugo's loathsome dog that was nibbling his shoe, a pug as ugly and evil-looking as Hugo himself. He had to vent his irritation and disappointment on something. After all, it had given him a fierce glow of pride to lie in the warm place hitherto regarded as the King's prerogative, and he was going to look a damn fool when the Wreckers came to hear of his downfall. How could she make use of him so, and then drop him once she no longer had any use for him in her little intrigues! It was monstrous!

Hugo removed the pug unobtrusively from Nicholas's reach. "You must put the whole disappointing episode from your mind, my friend," he said coolly. "You know what they say about spilt milk." Nicholas grunted. "You must distract yourself with other matters."

"What other matters, pray?" Nicholas snarled.

"A wench, mayhap. Someone pretty and diverting."

Nicholas felt like punching the creature's teeth in. He was tormenting him, Nicholas felt sure, knowing he had stolen the only filly Nicholas had really set his heart on this twelve-month. Chloe was Hugo's inseparable companion these days, and only one other wench had taken Nicholas's fancy as much as she, and that one had disappeared from Whitehall. Not once had Garnet been seen since the night she drove off furiously to Cheveril Street, the destination which she had cried to the coachman.

Hugo apparently misinterpreted his silence for consideration of the matter. "You have a wench in mind?" he asked, leaning back on the brocade couch and folding his hands behind his head.

Damn him for his insolence, Nicholas thought. Reclining leisurely there like a lord and quizzing Nicholas as though he were an inferior! Malformed little upstart! Why in blazes did Nicholas seek his company, anyway? If it were not for a possible position at Court, he could cheerfully put his hands around that gnarled throat and throttle that complacent smile at birth. Instead, he replied simply, "Mayhap."

Hugo smiled. "Keep your secret, then, my friend, lest one of the Wreckers should steal her from you. Unlike thieves, there is no honour amongst us, and it would be a challenge for someone of us to steal her away if it were possible."

Nicholas looked up sharply. Hugo smiled to see he had guessed aright. "So there is a wench? Let us hope she is fitting to play the part of the Queen of the Revels, for the next meeting of the Wreckers will be the annual celebration, will it not?"

So it was. Nicholas had temporarily forgotten that it would be the high spot of the year's activities for the Wreckers, a night of unusually immoderate drinking and debauching when any action was permissible.

"It is your turn to act as host, is it not?" Hugo reminded him. "So it is your prerogative to choose the Queen. If not, I know Chloe would be pleased to oblige."

Damn him! He was not going to have everything his own way! "Leave it to me," Nicholas said tersely. "I shall make all the arrangements myself."

The door leading to Hugo's bedchamber opened and a dishevelled, bleary-eyed figure in a bedgown emerged. It was Chloe, her dark hair still unbound and streaming over her shoulders, and her eyes red-rimmed and sunken. God, what a haggard creature she looked now, Nicholas thought. Playing up to Hugo had wrought havoc with her erstwhile beauty. Many pots of cream and lotion would be needed to disguise that raddled face. And to think he had desired her so intensely!

She yawned and rubbed her eyes. "For God's sake, Hugo, ring for some food and wine for me. I am starving." Her sleepy gaze alighted on Nicholas. "Good day, my friend," she said, and settled herself on the couch Hugo had just vacated in order to ring the bell.

"Have you selected a Queen of the Revels yet?" she asked Nicholas in an offhand manner, but there was no disguising the keen interest in her eyes.

"Too late, my dear," Hugo murmured. "He has a wench in mind."

"What?" she shrieked, and all the honey in her voice was melted. She gave vent to a stream of invective that would have well suited a fishwife, Nicholas thought privately, abusing Hugo and saying that he had promised her. Hugo shrugged and went to answer the knock at the door.

Chloe smouldered and muttered while Hugo spoke to the woman, and thrust out her lip sullenly when he came back. "Oysters and Canary, will that suit you, my love?" he asked. She jerked her gown savagely together over her knees and made no reply.

"You will join us?" Hugo asked politely.

"Thank you, no. I have matters to attend to." Nicholas rose, nodded and made a stiff bow towards Chloe, who ignored him, and went to the door. Hugo, as ever, was at his elbow.

"Take no notice, my friend. She is disappointed, but will soon recover from her little tantrum. She is a delightful creature really."

As Nicholas emerged into the sun-filled street, his spirits lifted again. He no longer cared a jot about Chloe; Hugo was welcome to her, and he wished him joy of her, but somehow he doubted if Chloe would be a joy to anyone. Now there was only one wench of any account to him—Garnet, the luscious, black-haired beauty who so far had eluded his grasp. Dammit, his mind was made up. He would have her and no one else as Queen of the Revels, by God he would! She would make the Wreckers open their eyes in admiration, in a way Chloe would never do, on stage or off.

In his mind's eye he could see it all, the revels and merry-making, and he would hold the event, not at his London home, but down at Yester Park, his mansion in the country. Only the finest background would serve as a setting for Garnet as Queen.

If he could find her. But of course he could find her—

111

Cheveril Street, she had said. If he had to take her by force, he would go to the haberdasher's himself and get her. No one but Garnet would suffice, and, by God, he would have her!

He strode home swiftly and gave explicit orders to Jethro for the morrow.

TWELVE

THE time had come, Garnet decided. Even Lady Catherine's patience would not be inexhaustible. She might even have engaged a new sewing maid and have no further use for Garnet, so long had she been gone. Garnet started to pack her belongings together again hastily.

It was then that she found the piece of rose brocade, lying on the floor of the press. Garnet picked it up curiously, then laughed. She had almost forgotten its existence, this remnant that had meant and symbolised so much for her. And to think she had mentally blamed Elise for stealing it!

Well, now she was on her way back to the glittering life for which the deep red stuff stood. She pushed it into the bundle along with her clothes, and went down to break the news of her leaving to Matthew. This was a thought she did not relish, for in his own quiet, considerate way he had made it clear how much he cared for her. And so had Daniel. To leave him would be heartbreaking. Garnet hoped he would still be sleeping in his cot.

Matthew was humming to himself as he opened the shop. It was a glorious day and he felt so lighthearted he wanted to burst into loud song. Trade was picking up again now. Customers had kept away from the shop while Daniel was ill, fearing the contagion, and the few hardy ones who still came had insisted on having all coins dipped in vinegar before changing hands. But now it was different. All was well with

Daniel and the world again. Any moment now, Garnet, with her light step and lilting voice, would be coming down to make his day complete.

He heard a step on the flagstoned floor and turned. Garnet stood there, her wide green eyes watching him.

"Good morning, Garnet," he said brightly. "Is it not a beautiful day?" He smiled, but she did not return his smile.

"Indeed." She hesitated, and Matthew wondered what was troubling her. "Have you eaten yet, Matthew?"

"Yes, Daniel and I breakfasted early."

"Daniel? He is up, then?"

Matthew laughed. "He could wait no longer to go next door and see Becky's kittens—her cat littered last week. He has been there this half-hour or more."

"I see." Garnet turned and fingered a riding-crop on the display stall. Matthew watched her, enjoying the sight of her slender, firm young figure. She looked so slight, so fragile, it hardly seemed possible she had all the strength and courage he knew her to possess. There was an air of great vulnerability about her. He had an urge to protect her, to take her in his arms. Not since Sarah died had he experienced this feeling. Garnet and Sarah had much in common, he thought, the same loving tenderness and quiet determination.

I' faith, he remonstrated with himself mentally, you're falling in love with the wench! Out of loyalty to Susannah, he tried to reject the preposterous idea. Garnet still stood there, silently, toying with the embellished handle of the crop. She had a lost, wistful air that Matthew found overwhelmingly appealing.

And still the notion of falling in love with her would not leave his brain. What of Susannah? he argued with himself. She does not care for you any more than you for her. And as for Daniel's plight, she would not even come to help. But Garnet—twice she had risked her life for the boy.

But no, he decided, it was not only gratitude he felt for Garnet, but a strong urge to cradle and protect her, to caress

114

and comfort her and shield her from all harm. He took a step towards her.

"Matthew." She turned at that moment and faced him, her small face serious and unsmiling.

"Yes?"

"I am leaving. I am going back to Whitehall. Now."

Matthew stiffened. All his tender feelings for her waned instantly. She had no care for him and Daniel now, but wanted only to return to the gaiety and glitter of Court. Why should he try to stop her, then, if that was what she truly desired?

"Lady Caroline has been patient long enough," Garnet was saying, "and I cannot exploit her kindness too far."

"I understand," Matthew replied. "As you wish."

Garnet held out her hand. "Goodbye, Matthew, and God be with you both."

Mattheew took her hand and kissed her fingertips. "God speed," he said briefly, then turned and busied himself with arranging gloves. He did not wish Garnet to see the disappointment that must be written so clearly on his face.

He heard footsteps cross to the door, then the sound of the door closing. For a moment or two he stood holding the gloves, then threw them down impatiently and rushed through into the parlour. There he flung himself angrily into a chair. A faint smell of jessamine hung about the room. Soon there would not even be that to remind him of Garnet.

Garnet closed the door of the shop behind her with a sigh. Whatever the fascination of Whitehall, she was strangely reluctant to leave the calm and pleasantness of this household behind her. But, putting the thought out of her mind, she hugged her bundle to her and debated whether to walk or call a hackney.

The door of the house next to Matthew's opened, and Daniel appeared on the top step clutching a kitten to his chest. He smiled broadly when he saw Garnet.

115

"Baby pussies," he said, holding the tiny, white creature aloft.

Garnet's heart melted. She had hoped to avoid seeing Daniel before she left, for this very reason. How unfair it was that a little creature could entwine itself around one's heart in such a way that one could no longer make rational decisions! She resolved to try and act as if she had not met him.

"Take pussy to show Papa," she said to Daniel, holding his arm to steady him as he descended the steps of Becky's house. Daniel looked up at her enquiringly, his dark eyes wide and serious.

"Darnet like pussy?" he asked.

"Of course I do, and so does Papa—go and show him."

She helped him up the steps, and then turned to go.

"Where Darnet going?"

Heaven's sake, this was the question she had hoped to avoid. "On an errand, Daniel."

"Tum back soon?"

Garnet hesitated. She could not bring herself to lie to the child. At that moment, however, the kitten sank its needle-like claw into Daniel's forearm.

"Naughty pussy!" Daniel admonished the creature. "Daniel tell Papa," and he turned to open the door.

Garnet took her opportunity and turned to go. She had barely taken three steps from the door, however, when darkness suddenly descended on her. Something coarse and heavy was thrown over her head from behind, and a pair of strong arms enveloped her tightly in the stuff.

Garnet opened her mouth to scream, and was nearly suffocated by the dust and the material being pressed against her face. She struggled and kicked, and felt the breath being squeezed from her body by the brute strength of the creature gripping her tightly. The only response to her heels kicking against his shins was a muttered curse and grunting noises.

116

It was useless. She could not cry out, and felt herself being propelled along the uneven cobblestones. No sound of life could she hear in the street, save only her captor's grunts and their shuffling footsteps. The filthy dust inside the sack was choking.

"Open the door," a rough voice commanded, and Garnet felt herself being lifted and dumped unceremoniously on a seat. She made to get up again, but was hampered by the sack and a pair of hands that firmly pressed her down again.

"Drive on," the same voice cried, and Garnet felt the seat lurch beneath her and heard horses' hooves clang on the cobblestones. It was evident she was in a coach of some kind, but movement or any attempt to see was impossible while the strong, rough hands held her imprisoned.

"For pity's sake, let me breathe!" she managed to gasp at last, and could have cried out with relief when the sack was removed and she was able to fill her lungs with air instead of dust. Beside her sat a huge giant of a man, a servant of some kind, with muscles like an ox and a determined glint in his narrow blue eyes. His hands were still restraining her arms.

"Let me go! How dare you!" Garnet cried.

"I will let you go if you do not struggle," the man answered, still breathing heavily from his exertions. Garnet looked about her. The windows of the carriage were curtained and the interior was dim. But this was no ordinary hackney carriage that plied the London streets for hire. It was well upholstered with cushions and curtains, and the windows had glass in them. It was a fine coach, such as the King himself used, and must of necessity belong to some nobleman.

The man's fingers had gradually eased from her arm when he saw she was making no sign of trying to escape. Garnet reached for the window drapes.

"Keep still!" the man commanded, arresting her arm.

"Where are you taking me?" Garnet asked. "And why? On whose orders are you acting?" She was no longer frightened, for the man seemed deferential enough and not likely to harm her.

"I cannot tell you, mistress. Only that no harm will come to you while you do not resist," he answered curtly.

Garnet tried to keep her wits about her. If only she knew which way they were heading, she could perhaps escape and retrace her steps later, but all she knew was that the coach was still clattering at breakneck speed along cobbled streets. Occasionally she could hear a shrill, protesting cry as some farm wagon was driven off the road by the huge, lumbering coach, and the crack of the whip as the driver spurred on the horses.

She listened to the hoofbeats. Four horses, if she was not mistaken. It must, indeed, be someone rich who owned such a coach and four. Lady Caroline she dismissed instantly. However much she wanted her sewing maid back, she would hardly send a coach and four to abduct her so unceremoniously.

Gradually she saw the man relax. He no longer sat so stiffly over her, but leaned back against the headcushions. That was good. If she could lull his suspicions she could perhaps later be able to catch him off guard and make her escape. But where was he taking her?

Soon the sound of hooves ringing out on cobbles gave way to a softer thud, and the coach lurched more violently than before. That meant they had left London behind and were on one of the roads out into the country. But in which direction? If only she could have seen out of the window she could have told by the sun whether they were heading north or south, but in the cool darkness of the curtained interior there was no way of guessing.

Garnet reckoned they must have been sitting there for above an hour. Still the man refused to be drawn, shaking his head in answer to her questions. Finally she gave up. It was useless to consider making a sudden dive for the carriage door and throwing herself out, hoping for a cushion of grassy hillock to soften her fall. At the speed the coach was travelling she would be lucky to escape with but a few broken bones.

The ride grew bumpier and more and more nauseating. After two hours even the man began to look uncomfortable, and Garnet felt distinctly sick and her head throbbed.

"For God's sake, let me open a window," she begged at last, "or I fear I shall throw up."

The man nodded, and leaned over to draw back a curtain and lower the window. Sunlight streamed in and lit up the darkness, and a cool draught of air revived Garnet and began to dissipate the throbbing headache. Through the window she could see fields and trees and an occasional stream or farmhouse flash by. But she still did not know where she was.

She caught sight of her bundle on the floor. The man must have picked it up in Cheveril Street when she dropped it. "May I get my pomander?" she asked. He considered, then nodded.

Sniffing the pomander of rose leaves and angelica, citron peel and zodoary that Lady Catherine had given her helped greatly in reducing the headache. As she began to replace it in the bundle, the coach suddenly lurched, hovered, and crashed over on its side. The man's weight fell violently atop her, nearly crushing her ribs.

"What in hell's name!" the man roared, and, forcing the topside door open, he climbed out. Garnet heard voices shouting and arguing, and peered out. The man was expostulating noisily with the coachman, waving his arms and gesticulating, and the coachman was surveying the coach ruefully.

"I couldna help it, Jethro. The wheel has come off," he said mournfully. "Blame the road, not me."

"If you had not been driving like a maniac it would not have happened!" Jethro roared. "Your mission was only to get out of London at all speed, not drive the whole way like a madman!"

"There's an inn only about half a mile away—mayhap I

can get help there," the sad-faced coachman suggested hopefully.

Jethro grunted. "Aye. I'll wait there with the lady till it's mended. Now make haste and get it done quickly if you don't want to suffer his lordship's wrath."

His lordship! Garnet was puzzled. Of course, it had to be a lord who would own such a coach, but who was he? And why did he have Garnet abducted? Jethro came to help her climb out in a rather undignified fashion, and she no longer had time to ponder.

"We'll eat and rest at the inn yonder till the coach is ready, mistress," Jethro told her, and set off to walk alongside her, each of his long strides covering the ground of three of Garnet's steps. Soon the whitewashed little inn came in sight, and Garnet felt glad to see its trim, neat-kept appearance.

Under the swinging signboard depicting a gaudily-painted red rose, Jethro stopped. "Mind you, now," he said to Garnet, "I can only let you enter if you promise not to call for help. It would be more than my life was worth if I did not deliver you safely," he added.

Garnet did not answer, but walked straight in, and Jethro followed her. The coachman was already haggling with some farm labourers over the cost of their hire, to lend their stout shoulders to the coach.

"Not a word, mind. I'll do the ordering," Jethro reminded her, and helped her to seat herself at the high-backed settle. Then he called for wine for the lady and ale for himself, and sat down diffidently opposite her, as if aware that it was not really his place to sit with her.

A plump-cheeked, country-fresh girl of about fifteen came to serve the wine and ale. "And what will you have to eat?" she asked, letting her eyes run freely over Garnet's figure and clothes. She was evidently wondering why such a modestly-dressed woman was travelling in an elegant coach.

"Venison pasty," Jethro ordered, and the wench whisked away into the steamy kitchen again.

After the meal was over, a perspiring coachman reappeared to announce that the coach was at last ready and fresh horses were waiting. Jethro allowed him a couple of tankards of ale before moving on. "After all, we're nearly there, lad. Only a couple of hours' ride. You can eat when we get to Yester Park."

Yester Park? The name held no significance for Garnet. The country home, perhaps, of the noble lord who had ordered her capture. But why was he having her brought thither? No doubt she would soon find out.

She followed Jethro out into the courtyard. For the first time she could see just how magnificent the coach was. It stood on the cobbled yard, its dark green paintwork gleaming and a gilded crest on the door. Its huge wooden wheels were clad in iron. No wonder the going had been so rough, despite the leather straps in which the coach was slung.

Four handsome black horses stood in harness, chewing the remains of their feed. She looked closer at the crest, but its crouched lions meant nothing to her. She still did not know who the lord could be.

"Inside, mistress," said Jethro, and he handed her up. From the inn door, the tavern wench stood watching them curiously, but soon she was lost to sight in the clouds of dust from the coach's wheels.

"Pussies?" Matthew roared with laughter. Truly, his son seemed to have naught but cats on his mind today. He realised this was the first time he had laughed since Garnet had left this morning and cast a greyness over the day.

"Yes, Papa." Daniel was standing facing him solemnly, still clutching the little white kitten to his chest. He had not let go of it all day. "Darnet go in big coach with pussies."

"Yes, of course, Daniel." The lad had cats on the brain today. He could seem them everywhere. There was no following childish imagination. He'd just have to humour him. "Garnet went in a big coach with pussies. I see."

121

"Yes, and a big thing on her head."

Matthew looked at him fondly. What big thing? Was he imagining Garnet a queen now, with a crown on her head? Maybe it was a measure of the lad's affection for her, to see her thus. He certainly loved her as he had never loved Susannah. And Susannah had made it plain she would have no truck with his sticky fingers when he was well, and still less when he was ill.

That settled it. He would write to Susannah tonight and suggest they break off their betrothal. He did not think she would break her heart over it, and his only concern had been to provide Daniel with a new mother.

But not Susannah, that was clear. Daniel would welcome Garnet, but she had other plans. But it was clear in Matthew's mind now that not just any woman would suffice to replace dear Sarah. If he could not have Garnet, well, so be it, but it could not be Susannah.

But first he must put Daniel to bed. "Take pussy back to Becky," he persuaded him. "Pussy is too little to leave her mother yet."

"Daniel want to keep pussy," the child protested, cuddling the kitten still more tightly until it mewed.

"When she is a little bigger you may keep her. But for now, let her be with her mother."

Daniel considered a moment, then made reluctantly for the door. Matthew tousled his black curls as he passed. Poor lad, he, too, missed a mother.

THIRTEEN

SEVERAL miles along the country road from the tavern, the coach drew to a halt again. Through the window Garnet could see a high stone wall snaking away into the distance, broken only by a pair of tall iron gates.

Someone came out from the gatehouse and swung the heavy gates slowly open, and the coachman drove on up a wide, elm-bordered gravel drive. Garnet heard the gates clang shut behind them. Sweet air scented with lilacs and honeysuckle permeated the interior of the coach, and behind a distant haystack Garnet could see a curl of woodsmoke rising from an unseen fire. It was at least five hours since Jethro had kidnapped her, Garnet estimated, so this place must be some thirty or forty miles away from London.

The coach crunched over the gravel and drew up by a wide, stone staircase leading up to the door set in the first floor of a magnificent stone mansion. Jethro handed Garnet down, and the beauty of the house, surrounded by stone balustrades topped with statues of nymphs, and long cool terraces, nearly took her breath away.

"We are here, mistress," Jethro said. "Yester Park."

It was a very appropriate name, Garnet reflected as she mounted the long staircase, for the house had a stately, old-fashioned air about it. She began to grow apprehensive again. Fear had vanished once she knew Jethro was not going to harm her, but now she was about to meet the mysterious lord, she began to wonder.

123

Inside the house, they came into a long gallery with chambers opening off. Jethro led Garnet to a panelled, nail-studded door. "This is your chamber," he said, and withdrew, leaving Garnet clutching her bundle.

She turned the knob and entered. It was a large, airy room overlooking the rear courtyard. From the window she could see the four wings of the house completely enclosed the cobbled courtyard, and a fountain splashed lazily in the middle. The far wing, the most southerly one, lay slightly lower than the one in which she stood, and the yard between trapped the heat and sunlight of the afternoon. Only the solitary oak in the vast yard afforded any shade from the sun.

Garnet turned to inspect the chamber. A huge bed, canopied and hung with red velvet, occupied one end of the long, panelled room. Deep, luxurious rugs lay scattered on the polished floor, and wax candles in silver sconces jutted from the panelling. A dressing-chest surmounted by a gold-framed mirror held a jug and basin. Near the window stood a handsome carved scriptor and, beyond it, a huge walnut press, ornately carved and veneered. A joint stool and chair with a carved back stood near by. It was, indeed, a finely furnished room, fit for a princess.

Footsteps approached and a knock came at the door. She opened it and found Jethro, now resplendent in a suit of braided blue livery.

"Is there aught you require, mistress?" he asked.

"No—save to know when I am to see your master."

"Tomorrow. You are to rest tonight, and he will come tomorrow."

"I see."

Jethro was still watching her. "Mistress—I shall place a guard to watch by you, so do not attempt to escape."

Garnet smiled. "That bed looks wondrous tempting, and I am tired. I am not of a mood for clambering over walls and then tramping the countryside throughout the night."

Jethro looked visibly relieved. "If you will give me your

word not to escape, then I will allow you the freedom of the house and grounds. If you will promise."

Garnet eyed him sharply. She could drive a bargain, too. "If you will tell me the name of your master, I will," she said.

Jethro's narrow eyes looked down thoughtfully. "I see no harm in that," he said at length. "It is Sir Nicholas Graveney."

Garnet gasped. Of course! She had almost forgotten Nicholas during her absence from Court and her preoccupation with Daniel. She could have laughed aloud. She had no fear of Nicholas. No doubt, abduction was his way of ensuring a quick seduction, she thought with amusement, but he might find that a little more difficult than he anticipated.

"Then I promise not to escape," she told Jethro, and he went away.

The headache was coming back. No doubt it was the result of the hot, uncomfortable ride, she reflected, and she felt stiff and aching, too. She decided to delay her exploration of Yester Park until the morrow. Although it was still only late afternoon, she would go to bed and hope the headache would soon disappear.

She slipped off her clothes, rinsed her hot face in the cool water she found in the ewer, and slid between the sheets. Their cool luxury was startling. To her amazement, she found herself lying between sheets of pure silk. She pressed her aching head into the downy softness of the pillow, and was soon drifting into a fevered sleep.

Matthew chewed the end of his pen thoughtfully. It was not easy to sever a betrothal by letter without penning words that could be misconstrued as cruel or hurtful, and the last thing he wanted to do was to hurt Susannah.

The shadows on the wall thrown by the firelight danced smaller and smaller as the fire died down. Moreover, the tallow candle was beginning to splutter to an end in its holder. He penned a few words hastily, and scrawled his signature.

Yes, it was better to arrange to meet Susannah and talk

about matters, perhaps lead her to agree that separation was best for them both. It was too cowardly simply to write and tell her it was all at an end.

He folded and sealed the letter, and left it on the table, then rose and carried the spluttering candle upstairs.

In the morning, Garnet awoke from a restless sleep feeling still somewhat hazy. The headache was still there, but considerably less in intensity, and her throat felt scratchy and a little sore.

When she swung her legs out of bed and stood up, she felt stiff and rather unsteady. Fresh air, she told herself, that's what you need, my girl, to clear a foggy brain.

So she dressed quickly and went to explore. She met no one in the gallery or on the huge staircase with the carved balustrade. Finding the door open, she slipped out into the grounds.

It was a beautiful garden, equalling the grandeur of the house. Below the brick-paved terrace, trim lawns swept down to formally clipped hedges, and around the house paved walks shaded by cypress trees led to shady arbours. Flowers spilled from huge stone vases, and there was an immeasurable peace about the garden at this early hour. Only the humming of the bees on their quest for honey disturbed the silence.

Behind the house Garnet found the stables and coach-houses and a dovecote alongside a pool, and a newly-planted orangery. Never before in her life had Garnet seen such magnificence, and she marvelled to think how wealthy Nicholas must be.

If she bargained carefully, she reasoned, it was just possible she could one day become mistress of all this magnificence. And even if Nicholas did not have honourable marriage in mind, which seemed more likely, there was still much to be gained from humouring a man so obviously wealthy. After all, he was a very personable young man. . . .

Half an hour's fresh summer air wrought marvels. Garnet

felt considerably brighter when she re-entered the house, the headache gone and only a scraping throat remaining.

Jethro was in the gallery, looking harassed and worried. "There you are, mistress! I thought you'd gone!"

"I gave you my word, did I not?" Garnet countered. "I have no intention of quitting such a fine way of life."

Jethro looked mollified. "The master bade me put all that you wish at your disposal. After you have breakfasted, I will show you the clothes and jewellery he ordered me to give you."

Clothes and jewellery! Garnet could not cease to marvel. What a fool she would be to decline an offer such as this! She knew she had chosen aright in leaving Cheveril Street and following the direction that her precious rose brocade had pointed for her.

Happily, she breakfasted on veal and cold chicken and fresh fruit from a silver bowl, washed down with goblets of Canary. She sat alone at the long oak table in the great dining-room. This was indeed a fine life!

Later she surveyed in ecstasy the gowns Jethro showed her in a vast carved press, before withdrawing to leave her to inspect them in peace. She squealed in delight as she fingered their luxury. Supple black silk, sensuous satin, stiff brocade, great puffed sleeves, and gowns sewn with huge bugle beads, silver braid and open lacework—there was every kind of gown Garnet had ever dreamed of, and some fabulous even beyond all her dreams.

She held them all up to her body, one by one, turning and examining her reflection in the long mirror. They were all so fine, so beautiful, that it was difficult to select one that seemed suitable for just passing a lazy day in a country house. Finally, she chose a cool silk gown the colour of a turquoise, trimmed with white lace at elbow and bosom.

She tossed aside her workaday gown impatiently and pulled the silk one carefully on. It was deliciously cool and scented. And, what was surprising to Garnet, it fitted her waist pre-

127

cisely, although it tended to lie a little too taut across the bodice. No matter, she decided, surveying her reflection. It displayed her figure to advantage. From the neat row of shoes she then picked out a pair of silver mules and put them on. She felt truly regal now.

She swept down the great balustraded staircase feeling every inch a queen. This was the life she was destined for, she revelled. How long would it be before Nicholas arrived to see her in her glory? She must ask Jethro.

She found him at last supervising the cutting up of great sides of beef in the kitchen. "When do you expect Sir Nicholas to come?" she asked.

"This evening, mistress," he answered with the air of a man whose mind was busy on other matters.

Garnet left him to his tasks and wandered about the house. Maidservants were flitting industriously in and out of every chamber, some carrying polish and rags, some carrying huge piles of bedlinen. Delicious aromas wafted from the direction of the kitchen the whole day. Garnet was puzzled. The house was alive with a swarm of busy servants bustling around in deep concentration. Surely all this preparation was not solely for her and Nicholas's benefit?

She tried to question one curly-haired lass who was hurrying in and out of chambers with jugs of water, but the girl simply mumbled something shyly under her breath, bobbed a quick curtsey, and scurried on.

All the servants, it seemed, were far too preoccupied to concern themselves with entertaining Garnet, and she was left to amuse herself as best she could. Not that she was short of diversion, for every chamber she entered revealed yet more and more delights, from cabinets full of curios from the remote East, to life-size statues of classical gods and indoor fountains tinkling into marble basins.

It was only as she thumbed through one of the great tomes she had taken down off a shelf in the panelled library, finding in it nothing she could understand, that her mind flicked back to the press full of gowns and slippers. Surely Nicholas had not ordered such a vast quantity of clothes for her, in the hope of seducing her? If he had, the plans for her abduction must have been laid well in advance.

Had the gowns once belonged to someone else? Or did Nicholas simply keep a collection there to please the whims of every doxy he brought down to the seclusion of Yester Park? Either way, Garnet's pleasure in the gowns began to fade. She was convinced now that they had not been specially ordered for her.

But what of that? she told herself defiantly. It was a gay, glamorous life she had been seeking ever since the day she had seen fair Frances Stuart in the Park in the magnificent rose brocade, and that was precisely what she was going to have at Yester Park. Nicholas would be glad to provide just one more gown in exchange for her favours—just one glorious deep rose red brocade. Garnet determined she would have that gown from him before even a kiss was exchanged between them.

Thus resolved, she settled herself to await his arrival impatiently.

Matthew waited all morning for the boy to return from delivering his letter to Susannah, asking her to call. It was afternoon before the lad came, whistling happily, and with no note in his hand.

"Did she not send a reply?" Matthew asked.

"No, guv. She said she would be too busy with her dress-maker all morning, but you could call and see her this afternoon."

The boy went away, grinning, and clutching in his hot hand the coin Matthew had given him. By mid-afternoon Matthew closed up and shuttered the shop, just as all the other shopkeepers were doing in Cheveril Street, for trade ceased early.

"Going to the bear-baiting, Matthew?" his neighbour the chandler called out, rubbing his hands on his apron thick with grease.

"No, I have business to see to," Matthew replied.

"That's you, Matthew Lambert. All work and no play. Do you good, you and your lad, to get out a bit and enjoy yourselves more. And the young lady," he added, with a wink, before going back into his shop.

Matthew ignored the jibe. People could think what they wished about Garnet's stay at the shop. *They* had not taken the trouble to help as she had; too feared for their own precious skins to venture into a house with a strange, unnamed fever. Dear Garnet! He had grown more fond of her than he had realised. The house was void and lifeless without her.

Jerking himself out of his self-pity, Matthew reminded himself that Garnet had chosen to leave, to return to the excitement of Whitehall. To have persuaded her to stay, to admit even that he loved her and wanted her company for all time, would have been to condemn her to frustration and possibly fretting. If, as he now began to admit to himself, he truly loved her, he would want her to be happy.

But still he must break with Susannah. He did not relish the prospect of facing her now, but it must be done. Matthew took Daniel in to Becky and left him playing delightedly with the kittens.

Susannah showed no pleasure at seeing him, but only relief that Daniel was not with him. She sat primly on the edge of her armless chair, her hands folded neatly in her lap. Truly, Matthew thought, with such fine gold hair and rounded face, she could be quite fetching if only she could lose some of the stiffness and that pursed look around the lips.

"Was it a matter of some importance you wished to discuss, Matthew?" Susannah asked, but her face had the faraway look of someone whose mind was elsewhere. The new gowns, no doubt, Matthew surmised.

130

"It is the matter of our betrothal, Susannah," he began, and at once he saw the interest leap to life.

"Yes?" she encouraged.

"I begin to fear, my dear, that mayhap we are not so well suited after all."

"Are you finding fault with me, Matthew Lambert?"

"Not at all. I simply feel perchance our outlook is not as similar as it could be."

"I think mayhap I agree with that."

Matthew felt a rush of relief. The matter was not done yet, but it had begun promisingly. He had half-feared that at the first indication of the trend events were about to take, she would leap at him in anger, and accuse him of betraying a woman's trust. Encouraged, he went on. He would not wish to burden her with the motherhood of a child not of her own flesh, he told her, but he felt sure she would grow to love Daniel as well as their own children.

Susannah obviously regarded the idea of numerous progeny with distaste. She joined in the discussion of her and Matthew's apparent differences in outlook with vigour, and before long she herself was saying that, in view of these differences, might she not suggest that to end their betrothal would be the best solution?

Matthew was overjoyed. So the final words had come from Susannah's lips after all! He felt so happy that, for the first time in his life, he could have hugged her.

They parted politely and still on quite friendly terms. In the vestibule, as he made to leave, the maidservant was just admitting another caller, and Matthew heard him say, "Master Felton presents his compliments to Mistress Susannah and begs to be allowed to call on her." The girl bobbed and went into the parlour, where Matthew had just left Susannah embroidering. Matthew passed close to Master Felton as he went out, but the handsome young man was too busy arranging his cravat and straightening his lace cuffs to notice him.

It was not surprising, Matthew thought as he walked back to Cheveril Street, that Susannah was not breaking her heart over a broken betrothal to a merchant. She had better prospects in view.

FOURTEEN

ALL day Garnet waited, resplendent in her finery and anxious to make an impression on Nicholas. But when the sun, having lingered in deep crimson glory, shimmered and faded slowly away and darkness crept over Yester Park, still he had not come. He was in no hurry to make his conquest, Garnet thought disappointedly. Waiting, he probably conjectured, might subdue her and make her an easier victim. But just wait; she would show him. She would drive a yet harder bargain before she succumbed.

She lay in the vast bed, willing the morning to come. Just after the longcase clock in the gallery had struck the hour of midnight, she heard running footsteps and voices in the hall. She rose quickly and listened at the door.

"Hurry, hurry!" Jethro's voice was urging other servants. "The master is here! Make all ready for his welcome!"

As Garnet scrambled into a quilted satin dressing-gown from the press, she heard the crunching of carriage wheels on the gravel drive. He was here! Her heart lifted in anticipation. Steady now, she told herself, it would be a mistake to appear too anxious. Make your entrance coolly and graciously, not like an over-eager village wench anxious for a tumble in the hay.

She made her way to the head of the staircase with stately grace. What a commotion below to welcome the master! Clattering footsteps, bawled orders, laughter—and female giggles. Nicholas was not alone, then, after all.

133

As she reached the head of the stairs and began her descent, Garnet saw to her amazement that the candle-lit hall was crowded with elegant dandies and bewigged fops, chattering women expressing wide-eyed wonderment at the magnificence of the house, maids carrying their mistresses' boxes —everywhere was alive and teeming with excited people. It was like the Stone Gallery in Whitehall all over again! Garnet stood stunned, only a few steps from the top of the stairs, one hand holding the carved balustrade for support. Suddenly she caught sight of Nicholas's blond head as he stood laughing near the door. He turned and saw her, and strode to the foot of the stairs.

"Mistress Garnet!" his voice rang out, and the din hushed as everyone stopped to listen. "I am honoured to have you as a guest in my house."

He made a low, flourishing bow and held out his hand to her. As Garnet advanced, he half-turned to face the crowd. "Ladies and gentlemen, may I introduce to you, Garnet, my queen," he said.

Garnet was flattered, both by his quaint phrase which implied admiration, and by the satisfying whistles and murmurs of appreciation from the men. A dark-haired woman broke loose from the crowd and came to stand next to Nicholas.

"You mean—you've chosen her?" the woman said, her voice hard and incredulous. "Good God—you're mad!"

Garnet recognised her then. It was the actress from the King's Theatre, Chloe, the girl she had first seen outside the tavern and who had threatened to scratch her eyes out. She stared at Garnet with glittering hatred in her eyes, and looked as if she might still attempt to carry out her threat.

A smaller figure detached itself from the crowd and came forward. Garnet recognised Hugo, Nicholas's hump-backed, card-playing friend. He took Chloe's arm, and Garnet felt a flicker of surprise at seeing this bent little figure holding the arm of a pretty woman so much taller than himself.

"Come now, my dear," he said soothingly. "We are Nicholas's guests. Moreover, the hour is late and you must be hungry and tired after the journey. Let me take your cloak, and if Nicholas would show us our rooms—?"

He looked up at Nicholas. Chloe snorted and wrenched her arm from Hugo's hold. Nicholas signalled to Jethro, who began leading guests away to their chambers.

Hugo approached Nicholas. "Take no notice of Chloe, my friend. She has imbibed rather too liberally on the coach, I fear. The heat and the dust, you know. Two magnums of champagne disappeared down her dry gullet before we even got out of London. She means no harm, I am sure of it."

He smiled ingratiatingly at Garnet, who shuddered. This vile little man gave her the same feeling of slimy repulsiveness as a snake. Then he turned to go.

Nicholas came to stand before Garnet again. He was smiling contentedly. Over his shoulder Garnet could see Hugo, still leering and grimacing at her, and felt vaguely disquieted.

Nicholas, unaware of Hugo's ogling, took Garnet's hand. "You look absolutely ravishing, my dear." He fingered the thick tresses streaming over her shoulders. "So ravishing you took their breath away, just as I hoped. Will you join us now in the dining-room while we eat?"

Garnet, stunned by the unexpected arrival of the crowd and embarrassed by Hugo's malevolent wink from a distance, shook her head. "If you do not mind, I should prefer to return to bed," she said, "and in the morning we can talk of why you abducted me thus."

Nicholas smiled and bowed, and Garnet re-ascended the stairs. God, she was lovely, he thought to himself, even caught unawares. He was delighted with the formidable impact she had made on the Wreckers—their unwonted silence on first seeing her was evidence enough of their stunned appreciation. It was best, however, not to expose her to public view for too long this evening. Let her be the subject of their toasting at the dining table tonight, and tomorrow she would appear more glorious still, decked out in the elegant finery he kept stored for his female companions.

And the crowning moment would come when she finally made her appearance in the costume of the Queen he had had specially prepared for her. But before that triumphant moment came, he had another joy to anticipate—Garnet herself, if all went well. For the moment, however, he went to rejoin his guests. Hugo was awaiting him at the door of the dining-room, where the other Wreckers and their women were already eating and drinking with gusto.

"A fine wench," Hugo murmured unnecessarily, for his comment was well screened from Chloe's ears by the din the Wreckers were making. "A noble choice for Queen, if I may say so. A lusty piece, too, I dare venture."

Nicholas ignored the question in Hugo's voice. He was not going to divulge that he had not yet taken the wench. Chance permitting, he intended to rectify that omission as speedily as possible. Instead, he led Hugo to join the others at the table.

Garnet lay abed, bewildered and confused. She was taken completely by surprise to see such a large party below. Somehow she had assumed Nicholas would have wanted the house empty save for her and himself. Then what was his intention in bringing her here, if not to seduce her? Or was seduction only part of his plan?

To ensure she was not taken by surprise again tonight, Garnet rose and bolted the door of her chamber. From afar she could hear voices below raised in raucous singing. They were evidently in for a long, roistering night of it.

Matthew took up his candle and went into Daniel's chamber. The boy was sound asleep at last, but Matthew could still see the tearstains on his plump little cheeks. Poor Daniel, he had sobbed unrestrainedly for hours when Becky's cat's tiniest and frailest kitten had given up the unequal struggle for life and died quietly and uncomplainingly. Daniel was inconsolable. The only person he wanted to sob out his grief to was Garnet, and he had cried all the more heart-breakingly when Matthew had had to tell him that Garnet could not come.

Matthew's attempts to soothe him had been to no avail. It was no consolation to Daniel at all that Becky's cat still had four other healthy kittens from which Daniel might soon take his pick. Mathew smiled sadly to himself. It had been typical of the boy to choose the delicate runt of the litter to adopt. He, too, had that overwhelming urge to cosset and protect that which was frail and vulnerable.

Matthew drew the covers over the child and left the chamber.

It was nearly dawn when Nicholas left the dining-room and went upstairs. Most of the Wreckers by now had left the table, either to go to bed or to continue their celebrations more privately elsewhere.

He paused outside Garnet's door, his hand resting on the knob. There was no sound to be heard but an occasional distant laugh or the tinkle of a glass being recharged. Should he make an attempt to win Garnet in what was left of the night, he wondered. The temptation was great when she was here, alone and unprotected, under his roof. But not so great as it would have been if he were not so exhausted after the journey down from London. On consideration, he decided he had not the energy to make a gentle game of conquest of it, complete with delicacy and finesse. If he went to her now in his present state, it would be but a quick tumble preceding a deep sleep. Not much joy in that, he reflected. Nor would she be very responsive if she were freshly awakened from sleep.

Still . . . He turned the knob, but the door did not give. She had locked it! Nicholas's first feeling was one of irritation. He was accustomed to matters going the way he directed in his own house. Petulance, born of years of having his own

137

way, made him thrust his shoulder against the door panel, but then he stopped.

Why should he damage his own beautifully panelled doors? Anyway, he really was too tired. Tomorrow, refreshed after sleep, he would enjoy her all the more. And this time he would take the precaution of removing all the keys from her reach first.

Next morning, Lady Caroline sat on the stool before her japanned dressing-box and watched Elise's reflection as she brushed milady's hair. Kate entered and dropped a curtsey.

"Ah, Kate! Is there no news yet of Garnet? Has she not returned from her errand of mercy?"

"No, milady," replied Kate, smoothing her skirt. "No news of her at all."

Lady Caroline saw Elise's lips tighten fractionally into a taut smile as she continued brushing more energetically.

"Gently, Elise! Tell me, do you know aught of Garnet?"

Elise's eyes snapped darkly at Lady Caroline's reflection. "No indeed, my lady. Nor do I care to."

"Do not be insolent, girl." Elise looked startled at Lady Caroline's unwonted reproof. "Then I wish you to go down to Cheveril Street today and enquire after her. Perchance the child has been taken ill herself. Go you at once and enquire."

Lady Caroline took the silver-backed brush from Elise's hand to signify her dismissal. Elise glowered, but milady was determined to teach the girl her place. "Quickly now," she said, and Elise flounced from the chamber.

Two hours later Elise returned, her face flushed with triumph. "She has gone," she informed Lady Caroline.

"Whither?" asked milady in surprise.

"I know not, nor does Master Lambert. He believed her to be returning to Whitehall."

"When was this, child?"

"Two days ago, my lady."

138

Lady Caroline bit her lip in vexation. It was not often she was mistaken in her summary of a person's character, and she could have sworn that Garnet was trustworthy and reliable. She was very disappointed, too, for she would have to search far to find such a good needlewoman as Garnet.

"If you please, milady," ventured Elise.

"What is it, child?"

"I found these in our room after Garnet left." Elise produced a pot of lotion from behind her back, and a small inlaid box. Lady Caroline took the pot and sniffed its contents.

"Rose petal," she murmured, "and my trinket box." She looked up into Elise's face and saw her eyes smiling with malice. "What are you implying, Elise?"

"She must have stolen them, milady, and did not dare to return." There was a complacent look on Elise's face.

Lady Caroline was shocked, and then her wits began to function again. Anger rose and flooded her throat so that it was difficult to speak.

"Lying wretch!" she said, and rose to her feet, sending the jar and the box clattering on the parquet floor. "These items were missing from my bedchamber before I even set eyes on Garnet! It was you who stole them, and out of jealousy you try to use them to blacken Garnet's name! Out! Out of my chambers this instant!"

Elise cowered under the fury of her words. "I should have you flogged," Lady Caroline stormed, "you cheating little thief! Get out of Whitehall this moment and let me never clap eyes on you again!"

She advanced on Elise, who turned and scuttled, wide-eyed in alarm, through the door. Lady Caroline rang the bell. After a moment Kate entered.

"Kate, I want you to dismiss Elise from Court today, with no money nor aught she has been given," Lady Caroline told her.

Kate's mild eyes grew wide. "Has she given offence, my lady?"

"She is a thief and would have branded Garnet likewise. Get rid of her this instant."

As Kate turned to go, Lady Caroline added wearily, "Kate, do you know of another sewing maid?"

"I have a cousin, milady, nearly thirteen, who sews a pretty fine stitch."

"Then let her be sent for. Garnet will not be coming back, it seems." Lady Caroline sighed, and she began to dress her own hair unaided.

Down in Cheveril Street, Matthew was giving Daniel his evening meal. The lad was still very subdued over his lost kitten, and Matthew himself was troubled. That pert wench from Whitehall had made it clear that Garnet had not gone back to Court as he had understood after all, and what was worse, the Court wench seemed glad of it.

But Matthew was less worried about the enemies Garnet might have in the service of Lady Caroline than about what had happened to her. Garnet would not lie to him, of that he was sure. She had seemed so eager to return to Court life too, so what could have happened to prevent her reaching there?

Then he remembered that Daniel had seen her leave, in a big coach, he had said. It was just possible he might also have heard Garnet give the coachman directions where to go.

"Daniel, you remember Garnet went in a big coach?"

Daniel turned his solemn eyes on him. "Darnet left Daniel," he said sadly.

"Yes, but did she talk to the man driving the horses?"

"No."

"Are you sure, Daniel?"

Daniel thought for a moment, his spoon poised half-way to his mouth. "Darnet have big thing on her head."

Matthew sighed. That crown again. "But did she talk to the man, son?"

"No, Papa. Man holding thing on her head."

Holding the thing? Matthew was puzzled. This surely could

140

not be a crown of Daniel's imagining—he had clung to his story too long for that. "What kind of thing, Daniel?"

The boy put his spoon down. "Big bag," he said triumphantly at last.

Matthew's heart stopped. A bag could only be intended to prevent her crying out. If Daniel was right, then by heaven! she must have been abducted!

It was unbelievable! Who would want to kidnap Garnet? And why? Whatever the reason, it could not be for Garnet's good. Matthew strode up and down the parlour, snapping his fingers and thinking. Oh God! How frustrating to be unable to do aught to help her! How could he possibly trace her now, after two days?

Daniel watched his father thoughtfully. "Pussies on coach," he added after a time. "Pretty pussies."

Pussies? Daniel had spoken of them before. Matthew knelt before his son and took his hands in his own.

"Tell me about the pussies, son."

"On the coach, two pussies on the coach."

"Real ones?"

Daniel looked at him and sighed. "No, not real pussies," he explained patiently. "Picture of pussies on the door."

Matthew leapt up. So that was it! A crest! Well now he was making progress. A crest could only mean a nobleman of some kind. But which one had a cat on his crest? Matthew paced feverishly up and down again, while Daniel went on placidly eating his meal.

Lions—that was it! Cats large or small were all the same to Daniel. It only remained to discover which of Garnet's acquaintances at Whitehall had a crest which included lions.

Matthew felt excited now he had something to work upon and began to make plans. He would leave Daniel in Becky's care and set about making enquiries without delay. He must trace Garnet quickly, for if any harm were to befall her. . . . He clenched his jaw firmly. Nothing must happen to her, or, by God, he would pay out the devil who harmed her. Even if

141

it meant a duel. Although he had never handled a weapon in his life, Matthew was prepared to take up arms and surrender his life, if necessary, to protect Garnet.

He bundled Daniel into bed hurriedly, made hasty arrangements with Becky to see to him, and strode off into the darkening street.

FIFTEEN

IT WAS growing near midday before Nicholas's guests began to emerge sleepily, yawning and rubbing their eyes. Garnet had been up and carefully dressed and coiffured since an early hour, looking forward with keen anticipation to the promised revelry, but not a soul apart from the servants had she seen until now.

Then quickly they all began to appear, and it was not long before their subdued sleepy murmurs changed to lusty calls for food and wine. Drowsiness gave way to reviving interest in fun and amusement, and soon the house was echoing to laughter and buzzing conversation.

Garnet was happy. It was like Whitehall in miniature with all these elegant satin-clad ladies swishing their flowing skirts and laughing behind their fans to tease their brocaded beaux. She saw many interested stares in her direction, but none of the dandies made overtures to her. Perchance they considered it impolite if she were their host's companion.

Nicholas was an excellent host, she reflected, there was no doubt of that. Mountains of food covered the long dining table—cold meats, succulent fruit overflowing from fluted silver bowls—and the servants glided discreetly in and out bringing yet more as the quantities showed signs of diminishing.

Hugo entered the chamber with Chloe on his arm. Garnet felt a shiver run down her spine. What was the matter with her? Did she really find Hugo's appearance so repulsive, or was she cold? Impossible, on such a warm day. A summer chill, perhaps, and that would account for the headache that still came and went, and the soreness in her throat too.

Such minor discomforts were quickly forgotten when Garnet caught sight of Nicholas in one of the chambers set aside for his guests' diversion. He was leaning nonchalantly on the back of a chair, watching a game of cards in progress. Several of the guests were pressing forward to see the game, and four earnest faces scanned their cards thoughtfully. Somewhere in a corner someone was playing the virginals, but its muted sound was obscured by the chattering voices laying wagers as to the outcome of the game, or conducting hearty and somewhat bawdy flirtation.

Nicholas looked up and saw her across the room, and he smiled contentedly. Garnet looked every whit as delectable as she had done on the stairs last night. He looked about him and was gratified to see others were evidently appreciating her loveliness just as much as he. Hugo among them, he noted, seeing the covetous gleam in the little man's eyes. Nicholas felt glow of proprietary pride. This was one wench Hugo would emphatically not steal from him. And the pale youth alongside him was wetting his lips with a pale, flicking tongue as he watched Garnet cross the chamber. He looked familiar, but Garnet had already reached his side before Nicholas could place him. It was Josiah, the ineffectual youth who had recently failed to qualify for membership of the Wreckers. Nicholas made a mental note to ask Hugo why the boy was here. Rules of the Club were not lightly broken.

She was half-smiling at him from behind her fan, her eyes tilted mockingly. God, she was desirable! For two pins he could take her right here and now, but even among the Wreckers some degree of discretion was the more usual procedure. He was well aware that at this very moment furtive stealing fingers slid beneath satin plackets, and behind

144

curtained alcoves more daring moves were afoot. Somewhere in this vast house one chamber must still remain empty, where he could find immediate satisfaction with her.

"I have a very fine collection of miniatures," he said, his even voice betraying no sign of the upheaval within him. "Have you seen them?" She shook her head. Without a word, he took her arm and steered her towards the door. It gave him even greater pleasure to know that Hugo was watching and would rightly guess his intention.

As they neared the door, it swung suddenly open and Chloe stood—or, rather, swayed—there, supported on the arm of an Italian-looking youth.

"Well, well," said Chloe with a slow, mocking smile. "It is Her Majesty herself—perhaps we should do obeisance, Francesco." She shook herself loose from her companion's arm and began to sink into a low Court curtsey, but wobbled and had to steady herself with one hand on the floor. She rose again unsteadily and glared at Garnet with malice in her eyes.

"And may I ask what spell you cast over His Lordship here to make him choose you for his Queen? Some draught slipped in his wine perchance, while he supped with you?"

Garnet watched her wide-eyed. Chloe evidently took her silence for inability to cope with her eloquence, for she jutted a hip jauntily, spread her fingers across it in a manner she was accustomed to using on the stage, and went on: "I am sure that witchcraft had more than somewhat to do with it," she said, "for Nicholas is not so blind he cannot recognise a face and figure when he sees it, are you, my dear?" She stroked him under the chin with her forefinger. "Why, it is not so long ago I could hardly keep him out of the tiring room, so obsessed he was with watching me dress."

She smoothed her gown from breast to hip slowly, her eyes on Nicholas's face. Then her complacent smile faded and she flashed a look of fury at Garnet.

"What have you done to him, you slut? You have nothing

145

I have not, nor, I'll wager, can you entertain the gentlemen as I can. Can you dance? Can you sing?"

Garnet regarded her coolly and made no reply. Chloe obviously thought she had the upper hand here, and every eye in the room was on her. She greatly loved an appreciative audience, and, true to her training, she reacted to that audience now.

"Come, boys," she called out as she swayed with a slow, lilting movement across to the marquetry table, where the card-players had abandoned their game to watch the encounter. "Come, let us show her what we can do. Roger, play the song I sing at the end of the second act—you know the one."

With the help of several willing hands, she clambered shakily on to the table, smiled round at the rows of eager faces, signalled Roger to began playing, and began singing in her shrill, strident voice.

Garnet watched and listened as Chloe sang, at first slowly and pointing every word, and then repeating it more quickly, waving to the crowd to join with her. The men clapped their hands to the rhythm of the song, gradually increasing the speed as they repeated the chorus, and Chloe, drunk with wine and intoxicated by the encouragement of the men, picked up her skirts and began to dance. She kicked her long, white legs, revealing glimpses of smooth, bare thigh that made the men whistle and call for more, and the card-players, who sat almost beneath her, made repeated grabs at her that she warded off, wagging an admonishing finger at them.

When she had finished and flopped down on the table, pink-faced and breathless, she was greeted with rapturous roars from the men, and calls for more. Hugo helped her descend, and she came to face Garnet.

"Well, Your Majesty," she cooed sweetly, "can you better that? Can you please the men better?"

Garnet saw Nicholas's eyes flick from Chloe to herself, to watch how she would deal with this situation. She took his

146

arm coolly. "You were saying, Nicholas, that you had some rare miniatures to show me, I believe?" she said, and saw the quick light of amusement in his eyes.

He rose instantly to her intention to ignore the trouble-monger, and offered his arm to lead her from the chamber. Behind her Garnet could hear the laughter of the Wreckers at Chloe's discomfiture, and Chloe's angry retorts. There would be more trouble yet from that quarter, Garnet guessed.

Nicholas led Garnet into a chamber which she had not hitherto seen. Japanned cabinets around the room held a variety of curios, miniatures and needlework samplers, but it was none of these treasures that caught Garnet's eye. Her attention was riveted by the couch in the centre of the room, deep red to match the velvet hangings at the windows. It was covered in exactly the same rose brocade as her precious remnant, upstairs in her bundle. She slid her fingers along the sensuous surface of the couch, and heard Nicholas come to stand behind her.

Nicholas flattered himself that his servants were well disciplined and the rimlock was as well oiled as it should be. There had been no sound as he turned the key in the lock. He slipped it into his pocket and went to stand by Garnet. Now they would not be disturbed. But no haste. He must begin by pleasant talk, to win her over gradually. A willing victim had far more delights to offer than a resisting one.

"By heaven, but you are a cool one," he murmured admiringly, snaking an arm about her slender waist. "You treated Madame Chloe as if she were of no account at all. It could have been an awkward moment for you, but you knew how to put that young woman in her place."

"I knew not what else to do," Garnet replied, still caressing the arm of the couch. "She had me at a disadvantage. It was all I could do, to ignore her and pretend it had not happened."

"Modest as well as quick-witted," Nicholas murmured. His hand slipped upwards, and she made no move to stop him.

147

She was just his kind of woman, he thought again, cool and intelligent, not boastful and loud-mouthed like Chloe. If only she would stop fiddling with the upholstery and pay attention to him!

"This is a magnificent material," she said, still looking at the couch and ignoring his fingertips on her breast.

"Silk brocade. I had it brought from Italy," Nicholas said. He was proud of his possessions, but just at this moment he had more pressing business. Trust a woman to shilly-shally when she must know why he had brought her here.

"I would give anything for a gown of this stuff," she said at length when his fingers had found their mark.

"Gowns, fur wraps, jewels, what you will," Nicholas slurred, drunk with anticipation.

"A gown of this very same stuff," she repeated firmly, turning to look him in the eyes, her own wide and earnest. "The very same."

There was unwonted determination in her voice, Nicholas noted. But if that was all she wanted, she was a bargain at the price. "You shall have it," he said.

Garnet wrenched free of his hands and crossed quickly to the window. Nicholas scowled and followed her.

"You promise?" she asked, with her back towards him. Promise! That was typical of a woman!

"Of course."

"When?"

Nicholas sighed. "As soon as it is possible. I shall give orders today, if you wish. Now come and sit with me." He turned her by the shoulders, and she came obediently back to the couch. Nicholas unfastened the jewelled clasps on her smooth white shoulders, and let her bodice fall, revealing the milky texture of her breasts. He buried his face between them, and marvelled that Garnet moved not an inch, but sat motionless like a statue.

Oh, Lord! She was one of those cold fish who thought love-making was a one-sided affair, he thought with bitter disappointment. Had his need not been so urgent, he might have been inclined to discontinue his efforts, but it was too late now.

His persuasive hands roused her not at all, except to rise suddenly after a moment and push him away.

"When you have the gown," she said, as she refastened the clasps, "come to me again, but not until then."

Nicholas could have howled with rage. Not since his nurse used to take a treasured toy from him at bedtime had he felt so cheated and angry. Was this chit of a wench holding him to ransom over a mere gown? When there were already dozens of the best he could procure cramming the closets upstairs? Dammit, she was not going to treat him like a child, to be humoured when he was good and punished when he was naughty. No woman was going to master him!

He seized Garnet roughly by the shoulders and pushed her back on the couch, ripping at the bodice of her gown again. It fell away, and Garnet stared at him with amazement in her eyes, then suddenly they flashed angrily.

"Let me go!" she snapped. "I have a headache and I feel unwell."

"And what of me?" Nicholas cried. "I feel quite sick with need for you. I have waited patiently. Now let me have you!" He clawed at her gown again, and felt Garnet's nails digging into his arms through his sleeves. He felt a glow of pleasure as his hands slid upwards under her skirt, but the pleasure was short-lived. A stab of pain in his shoulder made him stiffen, and he realised Garnet had bitten him through his coat. He roared and forced her head back on the arm of the couch, overhanging the small side-table. Then years of self-preservation by always giving tit for tat came out in him, and he sank his teeth into Garnet's shoulder.

She stiffened under his hands, and lay motionless. For a moment Nicholas revelled in the sadistic pleasure of his teeth in her flesh, then suddenly the feeling faded. She neither moved nor cried out. He might just as well be trying to conquer one of his treasured marble statues. She had no life, no spirit in her at all.

What a disappointment she was! Still, he might as well carry the business through, he thought. He raised his head to look at her, and an unexpected crash to the side of his head evoked a myriad fiery sparks, quickly followed by a fierce, throbbing pain. He saw the silver candlestick in her hand and the hot, angry flush on her face, and felt the writhing as she wriggled out from beneath him. He vaguely heard her wrestle with the door, then return to fumble in his pocket as he lay stunned, and finally the heavy slam of the door.

Roars of pain and vexation burst from his throat. Nothing was going right for him since he had come down to Yester Park, he almost wept to himself. Everybody and everything seemed to conspire against him. But he would get his revenge on Garnet, he swore it, for she was the cause of it all. Just wait—tonight's reckoning with her would be sweet. This would be a Revel to remember. If only his head had stopped aching by then.

He stumbled to his feet and went out in search of a cold compress for his bruise and some words of comfort.

Matthew was footsore and hungry, but he paid no heed to the demands of the flesh. Ever since last night his fears for Garnet's safety had been slowly but inexorably growing. No one had seen or heard of her, neither the neighbours nor her erstwhile employer, Lady Caroline at Whitehall, or so the liveried flunkey who had carried Matthew's enquiry to her had reported.

And so all morning Matthew had scoured London, even stopping strangers to ask if they had seen a dark-haired girl carrying a bundle, but they had all eyed him suspiciously and hurried away as fast as they could, evidently taking him for a trickster of some kind. Tavern-keepers had no recollection of a coach carrying a wench stopping at their hostelries, and Matthew was at his wits' end where to go next in an apparently vain search. By now Garnet could be miles out of London, and how could one pick up a scent two, nay, three days old?

But then Providence had relented and led his footsteps to Samuel's workshop, the old saddler with a face as leathery as the fine saddles he sold. He had listened attentively to Matthew's account of Daniel's tale about the coach with the crest, and rubbed his chin thoughtfully.

"Well, there's a crest or two as I know of," he said slowly, "with lions on 'em." Of course! Matthew realised with a start of hope that Samuel's work brought him in frequent contact with the horses and coachmen of the rich and noble.

"Who, Samuel, who has such a crest?"

"Let me see now." The old man rubbed his finger along his stubbled chin three or four more times. "There's Lord Chilton for one, the Duke of Hereford for another." He paused a moment. "Then there's the Graveney family, too, I think—yes, Lord Nicholas Graveney has lions on his."

Graveney! That name prompted a tremor of recognition in Matthew's mind. He sought wildly for what it was, and had at length a faint recollection of Garnet's having mentioned the name after coming home from Whitehall.

That was enough to act upon. He must find the house of this Nicholas Graveney at once, and here Samuel was able to help him.

Matthew hastened from the workshop with fresh hope. Long strides carried him quickly across London to the fashionable square Samuel had named, and eagerly Matthew climbed the steps of the imposing house of Sir Nicholas Graveney.

He rang the bell sharply and stood impatiently shifting from one foot to the other. Again he rang, but no sound could he hear in the large, silent house. Matthew grew angry. If Garnet, dear, sweet Garnet, were locked up in this place, then no pretence was going to drive him away until he had freed her. He was tugging the bell angrily for the third time when the door creaked open, and a slatternly, grey-haired woman peered out at him.

"Leave orf before you bust it," she snarled at him.

"I want to see your master, Sir Nicholas," Matthew said firmly.

"Then you'll have a long way to go, 'cause he ain't here," the woman snapped.

Matthew pushed the door further open. "Then I'll wait until he returns," he said, trying to get past her. The old creature resisted his pressure on the door, but finally had to give in.

"You'll have a mighty long wait," she sneered as Matthew pushed past her into the vestibule and looked around him. "'E's gorn down to his country house. All of 'em's gorn; there's only me left. But if you feel like waiting for a week, please yourself."

Matthew's spirits sank. "Where is his country house?"

"Who wants to know?" the old woman countered suspiciously.

"It's worth a gold piece to tell me." Matthew concluded that bribery would probably be the quickest course with such a creature to discover what he wanted to know, and he was correct. The old woman's eyes gleamed.

"Yester Park, down in Kent," she replied quickly, and her hand fastened eagerly on the coin Matthew held out.

Matthew wasted no more time on her. Another forty or fifty miles to reach Garnet yet, and by that time anything could have happened to her, if it had not already done so.

He made for the nearest livery stables and hired their fleetest mare. He fingered the sword at his side as he watched the ostler saddle her up. Please God Garnet was still unharmed, or, by heaven, he would run through the knave who had abducted her!

SIXTEEN

GARNET shivered both with apprehension and distaste, and tried to keep her mind on the lengthening shadows she could see in the courtyard below, and not on the assertive hands of the cold-fingered woman touching her.

Mistress Pugh had declared her intention of preparing Garnet for the evening's festivities, and would brook no opposition. Her master, Sir Nicholas, had given her express orders which could not be gainsaid. Mistress Garnet was to be prepared and made beautiful as the Queen of the Revels.

"But I have no wish to join the Revels," Garnet had protested.

"And I have no say in the matter but to do as I am bid," Mistress Pugh had replied obstinately, and proceeded to unfasten and undress Garnet. At a snap of her fingers, serving wenches had entered with a bath and jugs of hot water, and Garnet had submitted silently to Mistress Pugh's none-too-gentle ministrations.

Now, the bath cleared away, the woman was smoothing some kind of oil into Garnet's body. It had a strange, animal-like smell that was not unpleasing but somehow mysterious and evocative. That done, she opened a dressing-box that lay on the chest, and produced white lead and carmine. She painted Garnet's face and whole body with the white concoction, paying particular heed to trying to conceal the red weal on her shoulder, the mark of Nicholas's attention. She startled Garnet then by applying the carmine to her nipples as well as to her lips.

"I' faith," said Garnet in exasperation, "this is hardly necessary, as I presume I am to wear a gown, am I not?"

The woman laughed, a harsh, staccato sound, and snapped her fingers again.

"Indeed you are, my lady," she said, and one of the wenches entered the bedchamber again carrying a costume over her arm which she laid on the bed. At a nod from Mistress Pugh, she turned and left.

Garnet watched Mistress Pugh pick up the blue-green shimmering stuff and examine it critically, then, with a faint click of the tongue, she approached Garnet and slid it over her head. It was so light, so fine, that Garnet could see right through the material. From her training she recognised it for the purest, finest-spun silk she had ever seen.

When Mistress Pugh had pulled it down and fastened it into place, Garnet stood aghast, staring at her reflection in the mirror. Every curve and shadow of her flesh beneath could be clearly seen through the sheen of the silk, which barely covered her knees.

"There is an overgown?" she asked hopefully, and pulled vainly at the low-cut bodice to try to cover up her breasts.

"That is all," said Mistress Pugh, "and it is cut low of a purpose. There is a coronet for when we have dressed your hair, and that completes your costume."

Garnet sat bewildered while the woman's cold, deft fingers unbound and brushed her hair till it gleamed like the silk of the gown—if such a flimsy covering could be called a gown.

Satisfied at last, Mistress Pugh placed the coronet on Garnet's head and stood back to inspect her work. Garnet's dark hair cascaded over her shoulders and down her back, a stark contrast to the white face she saw in the mirror.

"No mules; you are to go barefoot," Mistress Pugh said with an air of finality. "Now you are ready."

"Ready?" Garnet repeated, the face in the mirror register-

154

ing stunned surprise. "But I cannot go amongst company almost naked. This is no costume for a ball."

"A ball?" Mistress Pugh's voice sounded as astonished as her own, and then she uttered the staccato laugh again. "The Revels are no ball, my lady, as you will see."

"Then what is to happen?"

The woman snorted. "His Lordship calls it a masque. Tonight it is to be the Judgement of Paris, he says, but, if you ask me, it is an excuse for the noisiest, most destructive goings-on."

Garnet was still puzzled. She had heard of masques while at Whitehall, but had never seen one. Did people really parade semi-clothed as they would never dream of doing normally? Even if they did, it was not going to prevent her from feeling embarrassed to the point of feeling sick with shame at the prospect of appearing downstairs like this. She must find some pretext not to go down.

"Pray tell His Lordshop I am still unwell—my head still troubles me and I would prefer to rest," she told Mistress Pugh, passing a limp hand across her forehead. It was quite untrue. For the first time in three days, the headache had left her and she felt perfectly well again.

"You could be rotting of the plague and it would make not the slightest difference," Mistress Pugh replied firmly. "I have been ordered to produce you at nine o'clock sharp, and I know better than to disobey Sir Nicholas. So come now, and I will take you to your shell. You are to be Aphrodite, the Greek goddess, rising from the sea."

"But I feel naked!" Garnet's voice was shrill with fear and shame.

"As I was ordered to make you appear. Come—no more delay." And Mistress Pugh took her firmly by the arm and led her out.

The large hall of Yester Park was teeming with men and women of every nationality, European and Asian, red-skinned

155

braves and black-skinned slaves. Nicholas was contented, surveying his guests in their varied masquerade costumes with high satisfaction.

His own costume, Nicholas felt, suited him very well indeed. He wore a saffron-coloured Greek tunic belted with a gold sash which matched his gilded sandals, and a gold fillet circles his brow. He was proud of the fine body he thus exposed to the general view. He was to play the part of the Greek, Paris, in the coming masque, and looked forward to seeing Garnet in her part.

Nicholas could see that Hugo, sitting opposite him, was also pleased with his costume, an elegant black satin suit trimmed with silver, and a black skull cap bearing two horns. He had dispensed with the customary tail that Satan was purported to carry, but Nicholas felt that, had Hugo sported the tail, his resemblance to a malformed monkey would have been complete.

The atmosphere around them reeked of ale and sweat, tallow grease and excitement, and bodies seethed feverishly about the table where they sat. Youths roared with pleasure, wenches quivered in wanton embraces, and hungry fingers picked constantly at the piles of meat and fruit on the tables. Red stains showed the path of jugs of wine to and fro across the tables. There was an air of expectancy, of pleasure yet to come.

Nicholas glanced at the clock. It was approaching nine o'clock. He felt a fluttering in his stomach and was surprised. Surely he was not so tense over Garnet's imminent arrival on the shell? He had given a great deal of time and thought to the arrangements for tonight's masque, to supervising the construction of the engine which was to draw the ornate shell into the carefully designed grotto, so surely he could not be nervous as to the outcome?

The quiver in his stomach ceased. No, it was not apprehension, he decided. It was more likely an over-indulgence in wine and lack of sleep that was causing his discomforts this evening, for he still had a stiff, aching feeling in his limbs and a throbbing headache. The latter was no doubt due to the weight of the candlestick that Garnet had cracked over his skull earlier in the day, and he could see that Hugo was eyeing the bruise on his temple with amusement.

Someone out of the motley crowd of devils, sea-nymphs and courtesans blundered against the table. Nicholas looked up sharply, irritation pricking him when he recognised the pale, vacant face of the youth Josiah. Josiah nodded apologetically, smiled nervously and vanished amid the crowd.

"What the devil is he doing here?" Nicholas snapped at Hugo. "He failed to qualify as a Wrecker. What do you mean by bringing him here? You must abide by the rules just like everyone else."

Hugo smiled his lopsided grin. "Do not excite yourself, my friend. He did in fact qualify after all, though he was scarcely aware of it at the time."

"Qualified? How?" Nicholas felt a stab of annoyance that Hugo had managed to sneak the youth into the Club without his knowledge. Hugo always got his way. Damn the fellow!

The ugly face continued to smile affably as Hugo recounted the tale of how Josiah had been among the group who had gone to the King's Theatre a few nights previously to see the new play. Chloe had reluctantly accompanied them, pouting and swearing because the main part had been given to her rival. Josiah, drunk to the point of forgetting his usual nervousness, had become bored with the play and madly attracted to the heroine.

"My dear fellow, you should have heard the comments he kept calling out to her," Hugo tittered.

Nicholas snorted derisively. "Everyone shouts out at a play. That's nothing out of the ordinary."

"But you haven't heard all yet. By the second act the poor girl was obviously quite ill at ease with Josiah's noisy attentions, but when it came to the scene where she lies abed,

157

bemoaning her lost lover and bewailing the fact that she must die a maid, it all became too much for our Josiah.

" 'No, no,' he cries, leaping to his feet and clambering wildly over the heads of the people in front, 'I am here, my love,' he calls. 'I will save you from a virgin's fate!' He never felt the blows of the angry people whose faces he kicked on his way down to the stage. He saw nothing but this painted wench waving her arms and calling for her lover."

Hugo paused a moment to wipe the tears of merriment from his eyes.

"Then he leaps on to the stage," Hugo went on. " 'I am here!' he cries, sprawling full length before her. The poor wench tried to ignore him clawing at her bedgown, and continued saying her lines, which was difficult for her with Josiah crawling across the bed and his mouth almost covering hers.

" 'Alone, alas, all alone!' she cried, throwing up her arms to heaven, but by now Josiah was between the sheets with her. 'What have I done that I should be treated thus?' she cries, and the audience was in uproar. Josiah's head appeared above the blanket.

" 'Take me, my love,' he pleads, then, 'God, don't you stink of greasepaint! Hold hard a moment,' and he leaps from the bed, seeks anxiously round the stage, and spots the new beaver hat of an alderman lying on the edge of the stage." Hugo clutched his scrawny belly, scarce able to speak with laughter. "Into this he promptly relieved himself." A tear trickled down Hugo's cheek.

" 'That's better," he says then, with an air of satisfaction. 'Now to business,' and he sprang back on the bed. But the poor girl had evidently had enough, for she fled screaming from the stage. Poor Josiah, he was very annoyed. Chloe was delighted, of course, at her rival's rout, and the audience was, too, for the moment. But when they discovered the actress was not prepared to play the third act, they grew angry and rounded on poor Josiah, who could not understand their displeasure at all.

158

"Scuffles broke out, and Josiah was obliged to climb into a box and thence on to a candle bracket. The candle fell on a lady's plumed hat and set fire to it. For a time pandemonium raged and the management had the theatre cleared."

Hugo cleared his throat. "A most diverting evening. Josiah certainly created havoc at the King's. I think one can with impunity call his actions those of a true Wrecker, don't you think?"

Nicholas grunted. He had completely lost interest in whether Josiah were to be allowed to join the Wreckers or not. He felt rather sick and dizzy, and was far more pre-occupied with his discomfort than with that stupid youth.

The long-case clock struck nine. Nicholas jerked himself upright and watched the drapes covering the recess across the chamber. Slowly they parted and swung back.

Nicholas was gratified by the sudden hush, followed by murmurs of approbation. There, in the recess, was a mag-nificent replica of a seashore grotto. Rocks carried in from the grounds of Yester Park gleamed under a cascade of water, shimmering green and translucent under the light of many candles. Great pillars of gold supported the central cave, where gilded dolphins bore huge gold urns of overflowing seaweed. Silver statues of whales and seahorses flanked the sides of the cave, and in the centre stood Aphrodite's golden throne.

"Magnificent," Hugo's voice murmured appreciatively. "Well executed, my friend."

"Wait until you see Aphrodite borne up from the waves," replied Nicholas. He wished furiously that this red mist would stop clouding his eyes. He could not possibly be so drunk already.

The murmurs of the crowd ceased as a whirring sound came to their ears. A giant scallop shell, propelled by some unseen engine, glided on stage and halted before the throne. There was an absolute hush at the breathtaking sight of this gigantic shell, lined with rich blue draperies and with coloured

159

glass simulating rubies, emeralds and sapphires sparkling in its dome. But the hush was not so much for the beauty of the shell as for its occupant, the lissom, dark-haired beauty clad in a diaphanous sea-green robe, standing proud and erect and aloof.

Every curve of her body, every shadow and gleam of her skin was clearly visible. Nicholas breathed deeply and exhaled a long, rapturous sigh. She was perfection. A glance at Hugo's ugly face revealed that he, too, was thinking the same thought. Garnet was the cynosure of every lecherous thought in the room.

The silence broke. Whoops of delight burst from the throats of the men, tankards were thrown down in haste, flirtations abandoned and wenches jettisoned from satin-clad knees. A fat monk, an eager light in his eye, clawed at Garnet's hem, reaching over a plashing fountain in his anxiety to grab her.

Nicholas strode across and placed his foot on the monk's ample rump and pushed him headlong into the water. The crowd screeched with yet more delight as he clambered, spluttering and choking, to his feet again.

"A toast," cried Nicholas, raising his tankard. "A toast to the Queen!"

Every man's arm rose and a cheer echoed round the chamber. Nicholas was sated with pleasure. An aged Neptune, trident in hand, helped Garnet alight from her shell and ascend the throne, while water-nymphs escorted her. The cheers still echoed round the rafters of the hall when Nicholas reseated himself with Hugo.

"A veritable Venus," Hugo was murmuring, "a right royal beauty. But so cold, so distant. Is she, in truth, so cold, my friend? Does she keep you still at arm's length?"

Nicholas was affronted that Hugo should have guessed. "Do you not see my love-bite, then?" he rasped.

"Love-bite? Not I. Where is it?"

"There—above her left breast," Nicholas snapped.

Hugo narrowed his eyes and looked again at Garnet.

"Indeed, now you mention it, I think I can see the mark. She is a wild one, then?"

Nicholas smiled. "Every wild colt finds its tamer one day, as she has in me." Hugo nodded understandingly.

The curtains slowly came together again, to the disappointed howls of the men.

"She will return soon, in the scene where Paris makes his judgement of the three beautiful goddesses," Nicholas called out reassuringly.

"Is that when Chloe makes her entrance?" Hugo enquired.

Nicholas nodded. "She is to play Pallas Athene, and Roger's wench, Daphne, is to play Hera."

"Does Chloe know the story of the Judgement of Paris?"

"I doubt it," Nicholas replied, "or she would never have consented to play the part of Pallas. She will be furious to discover that Aphrodite is chosen as the most beautiful."

"That she will." The miniature horns on Hugo's skull cap wobbled precariously as he nodded vigorously in agreement. Nicholas felt sick with repulsion looking at the ugly little beast, and had an inordinate desire to smash his fist into the rubbery, distorted face.

The fat monk lumbered into their table, his arm encircling the waist of that pale little pimp, Josiah. Nicholas's feelings of antagonism quickly switched from Hugo to the effeminate, pretentious youth.

"There is some time to pass before the next scene, so after your baptism of water, my fat friend," he said to the monk, with an air of joviality, "I think it is now time for the baptism of fire for our friend Josiah here."

It was gratifying to see the pale face turn several degrees paler. "What do you mean, Nicholas?" Josiah asked.

"It is a rule of our Club," Nicholas responded, and called loudly for his man Jethro. A few words in Jethro's ear, and some minutes later he reappeared with two other menservants, carrying a long iron tray covered with red coals taken from

161

the kitchen fires. Nicholas ordered it to be set down on the floor.

"Now, Josiah, you must run barefoot from one end to the other," he said.

"What is all this about?" Hugo's voice was sharp.

"Rule of the Club, my friend," Nicholas replied.

"There's no such rule, and well you know it." Hugo's voice was low but menacing.

"There is now, for I have just added it," Nicholas answered, equally determined. "Do you wish to ask members to vote on it?"

Nicholas saw Hugo's hunted look. The Wreckers were now all afire, scenting the excitement of a new sport, and nothing Hugo could say would deprive them of this pleasure. Hugo was no fool. He sat down again in silence. Josiah, white and perspiring, watched the exchange in terror.

Exultation filled Nicholas. He was master of the situation for the first time, and it gave him a sense of supreme power to be able to dictate to Hugo. Tonight the world was his to command. He felt like a lord of creation, with the power to deal out life or death at his whim.

"Then begin," he commanded. "Take off your shoes."

Josiah sat on the floor and began slowly to unfasten his shoes. Oppressive silence filled the chamber. Nicholas was irritated by Josiah's slowness.

"Quickly now, before the coals die," he snapped. Two or three of the Wreckers rushed to help Josiah by pulling his shoes from him, and lifting him to stand at the end of the tray.

His eyes were wide with terror. Hugo nodded to him, but the youth only swayed and looked wildly round him. Someone gave him a shove, and he stumbled on to the tray. His scream of agony ripped through the silent air and he danced, too maddened by pain to think logically, along the red path. Women shrieked and clutched their escorts' arms as a scent of charred flesh rose to mix with that of wine and tobacco.

162

Nicholas smelt it and felt nauseated. It reminded him of the time they had roasted a cat alive in a wire cage, and the odour of burning flesh and scorched fur had remained with him for days after. He leaned over the side of his chair and was sick.

Josiah lay on the floor alongside the tray, moaning and unconscious. It was Hugo who rose and ordered the tray and the youth to be carried away. Nicholas felt too ill to move or to care. He heard shuffling footsteps and murmuring voices as the Wreckers came slowly to life again, and within a few moments the drinking and carousing, wenching and card-playing were in full swing again, as if nothing had happened.

"Satisfied, my friend?" Hugo's quiet voice cut in on Nicholas's self-absorption. Nicholas retched again. Why in hell's name did not the ugly little beast go away and drown himself!

SEVENTEEN

NICHOLAS looked decidedly ill, Hugo thought. He poured another goblet of wine and pushed it across the table to him. "Drink this, my friend, mayhap it will help. It will be time for you to play your part with the goddesses soon."

Nicholas looked at him, but it was a wild, vacant stare, as if he either did not hear or did not understand. His face was flushed and the whites of his eyes gleamed redly, too, Hugo noted. It was not like old Nick to become so inebriated so early, or was the fellow taking ill, he wondered.

"Nicholas, are you well?" he queried. Nicholas rolled his eyes and did not answer; then, to Hugo's astonishment, he saw Nicholas's eyes waver and cross, each pupil sinking into its corner nearest the nose. It was a hideous squint, and Hugo wondered if his friend was playing a childish joke on him.

"Come now, my friend, drink up and prepare. I see Jethro looking for you, so the masque must be ready to begin. Come, Nicholas."

Nicholas's eyes slowly unknotted and reverted to their normal position. "The masque?" he stuttered. "Oh, indeed, the masque. Yes, I am ready."

He tossed off the goblet of wine and rose unsteadily, supporting himself on the table.

"Do not forget which goddess you are to present with the golden apple," Hugo quipped as Nicholas lumbered unevenly across the floor. "Remember Paris chose Aphrodite!"

Nicholas disappeared behind the drapes, and a few

164

moments later the curtains swept slowly open again to reveal the same ornate grotto and gilded throne as before. Three goddesses tossed a silver ball playfully amongst themselves, and Hugo could see Chloe, as Pallas Athene, was enjoying swaying and reaching up gracefully for the ball. It gave her every opportunity to display the curves of her fine body, only slightly veiled from view by the scarlet gauze tunic she wore and the thick blonde tresses rippling down her shoulders.

Garnet, her raven hair shrouding her face from time to time, threw the ball listlessly. A pity, thought Hugo, that she seemed so lifeless. A face and figure such as hers should have a fine, lively temperament to match. God, but she was desirable none the less! The sight of her full round breasts reaching out from her tunic inflamed Hugo, and he fidgeted restlessly in his seat. This was a woman he must have, whatever the price. And in Nicholas's present state of blank stupidity, drunken or not, Hugo just might be able to persuade him to part with her.

He stretched out his legs and enjoyed the sight of her. Strange, he thought, despite his disadvantages he usually contrived to have the women he desired. Being a secretary at Whitehall somehow blinded them to his physical shortcomings, and, he was proud to confess, he could usually occupy them so pleasurably in bed that they forgot all else.

He spared only a glance for Hera, the third goddess, played by Roger's wench Daphne. Too thin and flat for overmuch pleasure, that one.

Garnet's lack of interest in the game resulted in the ball rolling away into a corner. Pallas Athene, goddess of war, true to her stage training, picked up her bow and arrow and strolled across stage in military fashion. Her admirers cheered and whistled, but her solo performance was cut short by the entrance of Paris.

Nicholas came slowly but quite steadily across the stage, holding in his hand the golden apple. He stopped before the three goddesses, who by now were standing on ledges of the rock. He was still very flushed, Hugo noted, and there were droplets of sweat banded across his forehead.

Hugo watched with interest. He had told Chloe some part of the fable, that Paris would present the apple—a pure gold apple which Nicholas had had specially made for the occasion —to the most beautiful. He had omitted to tell her that the result was already predetermined by the story, and he knew Chloe was under the impression that the prize would be presented to the wench who pleased Nicholas the most.

So he was not altogether surprised to see her now, simpering and jutting a hip provocatively, trying to catch Nicholas's attention. As for Paris, however, his mind seemed far away from the beauties ranged before him. He stood as in a trance, one hand clutching the apple, and Hugo saw him suddenly screw up his face into an exaggerated wink. The goddesses appeared surprised, especially when Paris repeated the grotesque contortion of his face not once, but several times. Chloe recovered her composure first, and went on smiling and undulating gently.

Suddenly Nicholas appeared to come to life. He marched across to where Garnet stood, her face downcast and expressionless, and thrust the apple towards her. As if mechanically, she took it.

Hugo looked quickly back to Chloe. An expression of surprise on her face swiftly gave way to one of fury. The colour drained from her cheeks, and she stepped down from her ledge and ran across to Garnet.

"Give that to me!" she stormed. "You have received honours enough, more than enough!" Before Garnet could speak, she had snatched the apple from her, but so clumsily that it fell. Nicholas roared as it hit his toe, and Hugo winced for him. An apple of solid gold must be some hefty weight.

Nicholas's stupor vanished instantly. He rounded on Chloe like an enraged bull and made as if to strike her, but she was crouching low to retrieve the prize. "It is for Aphrodite, not for you!" he howled. "You shall not have it! She is the most beautiful!" And he kicked the apple hard, out of Chloe's reach.

Chloe rose, her face reddened now with fury at being cheated. "She shall not be so for long!" she spat viciously, and leapt on Garnet with the speed of a leopard, her talons spread.

Garnet shrank and covered her head with her arms, but Chloe slashed and ripped so venomously that the girl had no choice but to fight back or be maimed. Hugo sat entranced, unable to breathe, as he watched the two wenches roll on the floor, over and over, arms flailing and legs flying.

The Wreckers were enjoying the scene. They cheered and roared encouragement as the girls hit against rocks and blood appeared on their limbs. Hugo could hear wagers being laid as to the winner.

"Ten pounds on Chloe, old lionheart!"

"Fifty on the Queen!"

"I'll take you on—she hasn't a chance against Chloe!"

Hugo was too engrossed in the imbroglio to glance away and see how Nicholas was reacting, but he could see from the corner of his eye that Paris's saffron robe still stood motionless on the stage. Chloe raised her head, half-lifting herself off Garnet's postrate body, and flung her hair back out of her eyes. Hugo could see the Queen had made her mark on Chloe's face. Rivulets of blood seeped down the white skin. So the aloof girl was not so lifeless after all, it seemed. Hugo's desire for her grew all the stronger.

Chloe flung herself down on her opponent once more, but Garnet slipped quickly sideways and grabbed Chloe's long hair from behind. She jerked hard, pulling Chloe's head back till the muscles in Chloe's neck stood out like ropes. Garnet slithered round to kneel over her victim.

"Now," she said quietly, "are you going to leave me in peace, or am I to gouge your eyes out or garrotte you with your own hair?" Silence fell on the company, then one man cried out in admiration.

167

"She's beaten you, Chloe! Better surrender or you'll have no beauty left to delight us with at the King's!"

Chloe gurgled, then managed to speak. "You win; you can have the rotten apple. I can earn plenty more than that with my talents."

Garnet let her go and rose wearily to her feet. God, but she was magnificent! Hugo resolved to have her that very night, if it was the last wench he ever took.

If Nicholas did not prevent it. He looked at the Greek god, now walking carefully round the fountain where he had earlier baptised the intrusive monk. Garnet was bending over the pool, bathing her face and scratched arms in the water. Chloe had disappeared, no doubt to be comforted by one of her admirers. Money was changing hands to delighted cries of "I knew she could do it! That's fifty pounds you owe me!"

Hugo pulled forward a chair for Nicholas. He sagged into it, leaning his elbows on the baize-covered top.

"How fare you now, my friend?" Hugo enquired.

"Better, Hugo. But still somewhat heated and sick."

" 'Tis the air in here. You will recover soon. Might I suggest a game of hazard to pass the time a little while you rest?"

"If you wish."

Hugo produced a pair of dice and an ivory casting-box, and called for more wine. It would be best to render Nicholas even more befuddled, if possible, as soon as he could, making it thus less likely that his opponent would discover the secret of Hugo's success at the game. After all, Hugo planned that the stakes should become high before long.

Jethro set another flagon of wine between them. Nicholas splashed as much wine on the table as into his goblet as he refilled it and drank thirstily.

"Would you care to inspect the dice, to see they are square and true?" Hugo asked him politely. "Neither weighted nor set with a bristle?"

He knew he was safe in offering this, for this pair of dice

168

were indeed honest; what he kept to himself, however, was that the casting-box contained a hollow base in which lay another cunningly prepared set of dice, and which could be released by hitting the box on the table in a certain way.

Nicholas cast only a cursory glance at the proffered dice, grunted, and pushed them back to Hugo.

"Your first throw," murmured Hugo with every show of courtesy, and placed the dice in the box. Nicholas took it, rattled it listlessly and threw. Seven. Hugo took his turn and threw a pair of twos.

"The fates are not with me tonight, it seems," the little man commented, replacing the dice. "Shall we play for a stake? What do you suggest?"

Nicholas shook his head slowly and passed a hand across his brow. Evidently concentration was quite beyond him. All the better for his purposes, Hugo thought grimly.

"Shall we say my new carriage against your golden apple?" Hugo prompted gently. "Ah, no, the apple is not yours now, but Garnet's."

Nicholas's face was twitching again involuntarily, Hugo noted. What had come over the fellow? His red eyes seemed to register little of what was going on. Hugo smiled complacently. Out of the corner of his eye he saw a drift of sea-green chiffon as Garnet slipped silently from the chamber. This was going to be simplicity itself, like robbing a child of a toy.

"I have it!" He snapped his fingers as if the idea had just come to him. "I'll wager my Chloe against your Garnet. How's that? Winner takes both. Does that suit you?"

Nicholas moaned and buried his face in his hands, his elbows still on the green baize. Silence gives assent, Hugo thought, and called out loudly so that the other Wreckers could hear. He would need their testimony later.

He rapped the casting-box sharply on the table. "Nicholas lays his Garnet to my Chloe that he can beat me, you hear that?"

169

Buzzing conversations ceased, surprised looks came over the faces of the company, and bodies glided silently to surround the card table.

"Is it true, Nicholas? Are you wagering the Queen?"

Nicholas looked up and rolled his eyes. "Aye," he said weakly. Bodies pressed closer as Hugo shook the box slowly.

"My first throw this time," he said. "Ready, Nicholas?"

Nicholas's eyes were gazing at the baize. Hugo took his time about shaking, then poured out the dice. The hush broke. "Eleven! You win, Hugo!"

"Not yet, let us see what Nicholas can do." He scooped up the dice and banged the box down in front of Nicholas. "Your turn, my friend."

Nicholas made no move. "Come now," Hugo said softly. "All is not yet lost. Pick up the box."

As in a dream, Nicholas looked at him, then slowly picked up the casting-box. Hugo rejoiced inwardly. Garnet was as good as his, unless Nicholas were fortunate enough to throw a pair of sixes with the honest dice. He had the luck of the devil, of that there was no doubt, but he surely could not throw twelve.

Nicholas rattled the box, lifted his arm, and stopped, his arm in mid-air. The atmosphere was electric with anticipation. Nicholas sat as in a trance, motionless as a statue.

"Come, throw!" cried Hugo testily.

Nicholas's voice was faint, enveloped in his throat. "Can't —move," he whispered.

"What do you mean?" Hugo snapped. "Come now, stop fooling, man, and make your throw!"

A woman's voice began to giggle hysterically, and the tension was shattered. Men laughed coarsely and urged Nicholas to continue, hinting that he was afraid to throw after making such a boastful wager.

Nicholas began to tremble, his eyes staring wide and sweat trickling down his cheek. Slowly he moved his arm down, and

170

up-ended the box over the table. The dice rolled over and over, and finally came to rest. A pair of aces.

Cheers broke out. "Hugo wins the Queen!" Nicholas slumped across the table, and Hugo pushed back his chair and revelled in the approbation of the crowd.

"Will you take her now, Hugo?" a voice cried.

"No hurry, my friend, the night is yet young. Let us have more wine and drink a toast to the Queen, and to our gallant loser here." Hugo indicated the inert figure of Nicholas. "Though I think he is in no state to join us."

Ribald laughter brought the atmosphere back to its earlier merriment. Hugo drank deeply and with great contentment, but not so deeply that he would become unable to enjoy what the night had yet in store for him. He wanted to savour every moment of his triumph and of Garnet's charms. God, but she was a wench worth laying!

Garnet sat weeping bitterly in her chamber. What a night of shame and embarrassment she had endured! What a fool she had been to believe that Nicholas and riches were hers for the asking! She wanted only to quit this dreadful house and all its ghoulish occupants as quickly as she could. She had heard from Mistress Pugh of the terrible suffering they had inflicted tonight on some poor youth who in all probability would never walk again as a result. What vile, what loathsome creatures they all were, and Nicholas was the leader of their misdeeds.

Voices whispering outside the door caught her attention. It was a couple of maidservants. Garnet listened.

"And now Sir Nicholas has lost his Queen to the little dwarf," one of them was saying, "in a game of hazard." There were delighted giggles beyond the door. "He plans to take his prize tonight, he says."

The other maid shrieked. "I wouldn't be Mistress Garnet for the world!" she cried.

"Hush!" said the first. "She'll hear you!"

171

Garnet felt sick with horror and shame. Nicholas had wilfully wagered and lost her to that ugly little Hugo! How dare he! What right had he to deal with her as if she were a horse or a jewel?

Anger rose inside her, and Garnet determined to cheat both men of their wager. Neither one should have her, ever, she vowed. She locked the door of her chamber and withdrew the key, dressed herself in her own clothes, and slipped the key into the bodice of her gown.

Carefully then she bathed her wounds. Luckily, she had suffered only scratches. Then she sat down to plan and wait.

If the opportunity to escape did not arise, she would rather sit here and starve than open the door to anyone, and especially that lecherous little toad Hugo or that selfish, deceitful Nicholas!

EIGHTEEN

HUGO, sated with wine and food, heard the clock strike midnight and decided he had waited long enough. He nudged Nicholas's prostrate figure, still sprawled across the card table where he had fallen at the end of their game. Nicholas did not move. His was only one of many inebriated bodies lying about the chamber.

Hugo gripped his shoulder and rolled him over. "Come now, my friend, 'twould be better to sleep off your stupor in the comfort of a bed. I shall call Jethro for you, then bid you good night."

Still Nicholas made no response. His eyes were closed and his breathing heavy and stertorous, his mouth lolling open. There were small red pinpricks on his skin, almost concealed by the angry red flush. Hugo poked a finger in Nicholas's cheek and found his skin was burning hot to the touch.

"Jethro!" the dwarf called out loudly, and as Jethro came instantly from out of nowhere he said, "I fear your master is ill. It seems he has a fever. See you to him, man, for I am for my bed."

Jethro put his powerful shoulder under the arm of the unconscious Nicholas and heaved him to his feet. A passing Saracen, his arm about a tow-haired milkmaid, smiled. "Nicholas has had his fill, eh? Then he will miss the best part of the evening, I fear, for soon it will be time for the love-feast, eh, my pretty?" The milkmaid dimpled and giggled.

Jethro started to move away, staggering under the weight

173

of his burden, but suddenly he stopped. Hugo saw that Nicholas's eyes were open now and he was struggling to release himself from Jethro's powerful hold.

He glared, his eyes red and bloodshot, at his would-be helper. "How dare you attack me!" he roared, and like a maddened bull he put his head down and butted Jethro in the stomach.

"Jethro is helping you to bed," Hugo protested mildly. Nicholas rounded on him.

"You are in the conspiracy, too!" he roared, and dealt the hunchback a ferocious blow to his mouth. Hugo crumpled and fell. Others of the Wreckers gathered around Nicholas, who was swaying and waving his arms, challenging them all to try and take him.

His eyes rolled wantonly, as if no longer under his control, and slaver ran from his lips. The Wreckers wavered and fell back. The man was obviously out of his mind. Hugo rose clumsily to his feet and tried to slink away through the crowd, but Nicholas suddenly let out a tremendous scream, fell and writhed on the floor, clutching his guts and foam gathering about his lips.

"He's mad!" a woman's voice cried hysterically.

"Possessed, maybe," came a fearful suggestion.

"Poisoned, more like," muttered another.

Jethro bent over his master, then straightened, fear blanketing his eyes. " 'Tis the plague!" he whispered, then turned and ran, terrified, from the chamber.

The news hissed through the crowd, whispers of fear growing into whimpers of terror.

Hugo's stomach tightened. The man was right. If not the plague, then some other terrible contagion, for Nicholas had all the marks of approaching death upon him as he writhed convulsively on the floor, turning purple with the fever and the fiery red spots glowing on his skin.

The space around Nicholas grew rapidly wider as the Wreckers and their wenches slunk or ran from the room. Soon

174

only Hugo was left, rooted to the floor in terror. Nicholas had stopped writhing and was lying still, his tongue lolling out, white and swollen, and dried foam flecking his lips. His eyes squinted hideously, but finally managed to focus on Hugo.

"Help—me," a strangled voice issued from the lips.

Hugo, terror-stricken, turned and fled. Nothing on earth would keep him in a house of death. He must get out and away from Yester Park instantly.

Evidently the other Wreckers were bent on the same intent, for the passages were choked with people flying hither and thither, calling out, "Plague! Run for your lives!" and grabbing their most treasured possessions. Hastily packed bags, their contents hanging out through the cracks, stood scattered in the vestibule. Doors slammed and footsteps scurried in dread. Chloe, white-faced and trembling, came rushing down the stairs and clutched at Hugo's arm.

"Your coach, man, quick! Let us leave here instantly!" she gasped. "For God's sake, move!" Bodies pushed and fought to get to the door. Voices moaned and cried out. Roger's voice rose above the din.

"There's an inn some miles up the London road, the Rose Tavern. Let us all meet there!"

Hugo turned and ran for the coach-house, with Chloe hard at his heels.

It was nearing dawn when the little whitewashed inn came in sight. Matthew had no need to rein in his horse, for the poor jade was practically dropping from fatigue already, so hard he had ridden her all these miles. Her flanks were lathered in foam and sweat, and now she was beginning to go lame.

The signboard creaked in the night breeze. Matthew barely noticed the name of the Rose Tavern as he dismounted and strode to the inn door. The innkeeper, candle in hand, admitted him sleepily, regretted that he had no horse to hire out, but offered Matthew a cold meal and a bed for the night.

175

It was another ten miles to Yester Park, mine host told him. Matthew hesitated. Every bit of his body ached from so many hours in the saddle, and his stomach seemed to be tied in a cramp-like knot from hunger. He was sorely tempted to eat and sleep for a couple of hours while the mare also fed and rested.

"See to my horse," he told the innkeeper, "and meanwhile I shall eat." The host woke up the ostler, a lad who lay sleeping by the fire, and sent him out into the yard. Matthew tossed off a tankard of cool ale gratefully, and then ate ravenously when the innkeeper reappeared with a platter of cold meat and cheese.

The boy returned from the stables. "She's hurt her fetlock," he announced with a yawn. "Not fit for riding, she ain't."

"Will she carry me ten miles?" Matthew asked him.

The boy shrugged. "She might, and then again she might not." He eyed Matthew consideringly. "Could be I could arrange to borrow a horse from a farmer friend of mine, if you're so anxious," he said. The innkeeper was out of earshot, so the lad deemed it safe to continue. "Might cost you heavy, mind, but if your journey is urgent . . ."

Matthew produced some coins instantly. The boy's hand darted to the table, picked them up and secreted them in his pocket quick as a flash.

"At first light," he promised. "I'll wake you when I have it," and he disappeared into the kitchen.

Matthew accepted the innkeeper's offer of a bed, and lay down on the feather mattress without undressing. He wanted to be ready to go the instant the horse was brought.

Garnet lay apprehensively on her bed fully dressed. Every moment since she had locked the door, she had expected to hear Nicholas or Hugo knock and demand entrance, but so far not a soul had come near. Still she lay tense, for she knew one of them would come eventually to claim her, and she could not bear the thought of either one near her.

Soon after the clock had struck midnight she heard the noise of the revellers suddenly increase in volume. Footsteps pounded up and down the corridors and voices cried out. They must have reached the climax of the night's carousing, she decided, and buried her head under the pillow to shut out the din.

Doors slammed and the pandemonium raged for some time, then suddenly it died away and all fell silent. Garnet grew anxious. If the orgy were ended, surely Hugo or Nicholas would come now?

But time passed and not a sound did she hear. Finally, worn out from waiting tensely, she dozed off to sleep.

When she awoke, it was dawn. Still the vast house lay silent. The revellers were no doubt sleeping off their self-indulgence, she thought, Hugo and Nicholas among them. She rose and packed her belongings together again in a bundle, ready for when an opportune moment to escape might arise.

As she fingered the piece of rose brocade a feeling of revulsion came up in her throat. Strange, she thought, that for so long she had been led by dreams of magnificent gowns and wealth, given birth by this remnant. Now, after staying in this house with its terrible occupants, the dreams were revealed for what they were, shallow, vain illusions. She would trade them all willingly for the warmth and security of a life with love and tenderness in it, such as she had known with Matthew and Daniel. What a fool she had been to forsake that life!

She stuffed the material carelessly into the bundle and then sat down again to wait.

Nicholas opened his eyes. Not a soul was in the great hall but himself. The selfish creatures! They had all gone off and left him alone and helpless.

Pain was gnawing every inch of his body. He tried to rise, and felt as weak as a newborn kitten. With great difficulty he levered himself up by means of the table leg and lurched across to another table nearer the door. His eyes could not focus properly, and the whole chamber swam about him. In a brief moment of lucidity he wrenched the door open and fell out into the corridor.

He lay motionless for a moment, the mist swirling before his eyes again. Clumsily he rolled over and crawled on his hands and knees, trying to call out for help, but all that came from his throat was a cracked gurgle. Where were they all, damn them? No thought for anyone but themselves, and he so ill.

He found himself at the open doorway of the chamber where he kept his miniatures. There was a bell by the couch —he could ring for Jethro. It took years, it seemed, to crawl and flounder clumsily to the couch, where he lay breathless, retching and wracked with cramp for several moments before he could pull himself painfully up on to it. Then suddenly all his limbs seemed to lock rigidly and he could not move a muscle. The bell rope hung tantalisingly within reach, but he could not lift his arm.

Black mists swirled about him for a moment, then advanced and closed in on him.

Matthew had not meant to sleep, but when rumbling wheels in the inn yard below caused him to open his eyes, he realised that he had been sleeping.

He leapt instantly to his feet. Dawn was breaking. He cursed. He had no business to succumb to his fatigue until Garnet's safety was assured. He grabbed up his cloak and hastened downstairs.

The tavern, to his amazement, was crowded with noisy, cloaked people clamouring for attention, and the bewildered innkeeper was clucking around them fussily.

"Yes, yes, I can accommodate you all in time, ladies and gentlemen, but give me leave to call my good wife and the maids. Yes, I have beds a-plenty," he said, and then checked himself when he saw yet more guests were entering the door.

Matthew took the man's arm and led him aside to settle his reckoning. The innkeeper miscounted the change in his anxiety to deal with the newcomers, apologised to Matthew and made haste to explain. "Forgive me, sir. I am somewhat befuddled. So many guests all at once." He counted the coins again. "There you are, sir, I think that is correct."

"Has the ostler brought my horse?" Matthew asked him.

"Your horse? I know not, sir. He is busy outside with all these coaches from Yester Park. You had better ask him yourself, sir. Dear me, sad business. All this commotion because they fear the plague."

Matthew's ears had been caught by the mention of Yester Park. "What's that?" he demanded. "Plague?"

"So they say, sir. At Yester Park. Forgive me, sir, but I must go wake my wife and the servants," and he was gone.

Matthew looked about him at the oddly assorted characters who had entered the inn. Monks and libertines, nuns and courtesans, all of them wore masquerade costumes. They must have left Yester Park in a great hurry to be still thus strangely attired for a journey. A cloaked woman whose face looked familiar to him stood hugging the arm of an unpleasant-looking dwarf clad in black satin. It was the actress he had seen at the King's Theatre the night he had taken Garnet to see the play.

And Garnet herself—if everyone had fled from Yester Park, then she must be among this throng somewhere. His anxious look ranged across the assembly, but he could not see her. He decided to speak to the actress.

"Your pardon, mistress," he said, as politely as his anxiety would permit. "I am here in search of Mistress Garnet Appleby. Can you tell me if she is among your company?"

"I know not where she is, nor do I care," the young woman's voice rose shrilly. "Hugo, some wine, if you please, or I swear I shall swoon."

"At once, my dear." The dwarf patted her arm reassuringly.

"But was she with you at Yester Park?" Matthew persisted.

179

"She was," the dwarf replied.

"And where is she now?"

The dwarf shrugged. "Mayhap she is in one of the coaches that follows and has yet to arrive. I fear we left in rather too much of a hurry to account for all our number. The plague, you know, distracted us."

"Then Sir Nicholas Graveney—can you tell me where I may find him?" Matthew asked, growing more and more afraid for Garnet each moment.

"Indeed." The dwarf's malevolent eyes seemed positively to smile with pleasure. "He is yet at Yester Park. He is the reason we fled so precipitately."

Matthew stared in disbelief. "You mean—it is Sir Nicholas who is stricken with the plague?"

The dwarf nodded. "Or some illness remarkably akin to it."

The actress frowned sharply. "Hugo, my wine," she reminded him. The dwarf went off in search of it.

Matthew gasped in horror. Nicholas had taken Garnet to Yester Park, and now she was missing, possibly left behind, the only person to care for him.

He raced out into the inn yard, snatched a horse from the ostler who was about to unsaddle it, and galloped headlong towards the sunrise.

It was broad daylight now, and still Garnet had not heard one sound to break the silence of Yester Park. From her window she had seen no one, not even a servant, cross the courtyard below.

It was strange, she thought. One could expect to hear servants moving about even though their masters and mistresses still slept. And now she came to think of it, there had been no scent of cooking rising from the kitchens across the yard. She opened her windows and sniffed. No, not a drift of roasting or even of woodsmoke could she detect.

She strained hard, craning her neck around until she could just see into the coach-house window. There was no sign of any of the carriages, nor could she hear the sound of horses neighing or trampling.

Had everyone in the house suddenly been spirited away in the night? Was the mansion really deserted? Or, the thought came to her, was it simply some trick of Nicholas's clever devising to deceive her into believing everyone gone, just to tempt her to come out of hiding?

She sat on the huge bed, hugged her bundle to her, and debated what to do. If she took a chance and tried to sneak out she might walk straight into a trap. On the other hand, she could sit here alone for ever and no one would ever know.

She would have to come out sooner or later. Best to make sure first, though, that there was no snare. She decided to wait a little longer.

NINETEEN

MATTHEW rode like one possessed. At a fork in the road he reined in. A fallen signpost lay askew, leaning drunkenly on a hedge as if for support. Matthew swore. At a time like this, to find the signpost uprooted, possibly by one of those carriages which had recently sped this way in too much haste to care about aught but distance and safety!

There was no time to lose. He must reach Garnet quickly. There was no dwelling in sight at which he could enquire the way to Yester Park. He chose the road to the left and dug his heels hard into the horse's flanks.

After a mile or two of gentle, undulating plains, he reckoned he must have covered at least nine or ten miles since leaving the Rose Tavern, but still there was no sign of the Park. A hill lay ahead of him. He drove his horse relentlessly to the top and paused on the crest to look about him.

There was no house ahead for the next few miles. Hellfire! He must have taken the wrong road back at the fork, after all! He jerked the horse about savagely and galloped back the way he had come.

Dear God, he prayed, let no harm have come to her!

All kinds of strange thoughts had been going through Garnet's mind while she sat and waited. She had been thinking how differently Nicholas had turned out from the amiably lazy youth she had taken him for in Hyde Park, and, for no reason at all, a pair of magnetically intense eyes, blue and unwavering, had come into her mind. Then she placed them as those of the old crone in the Park.

What was it the old woman had said? That there was danger for Garnet if she stayed. That what Garnet saw there that day would lead to evil, she had prophesied. Had she perchance been referring to Nicholas? Or possibly to the rose brocade gown that Lady Frances Stuart wore? Both had been instrumental in bringing Garnet to this dreadful place.

Garnet was mildly surprised to find that the rose brocade stirred no feelings in her any more. To think that all this time she had been led only by dreams of all that this scrap stood for, and now it meant nothing to her. She had been a fool. Misguided by her ambition, she had overlooked what had been truly good and worth while. She remembered fondly baby Daniel's quiet trust in her and his undemanding love, and, remembering him, she saw in him his father's eyes, serious and considerate, tender and concerned. Dear Matthew. Him, too, she had rejected when he had offered her a home and comfort. She must have been demented by her ruthless craving. What a blind, stupid, thoughtless idiot she had been!

The next thought that struck her was where could she possibly go if she did manage to escape from this place? Madame Barin and Reginald Baskcomb were part of a past life to which she could never return even if she wished. Lady Caroline would by now have given up hope of her coming back to Whitehall, and would doubtless have employed another sewing maid in her place. And after her selfish treatment of Matthew, she could hardly go back and seek shelter there.

Garnet began to feel very lonely and, for the first time, very frightened. A dog howled somewhere in the distance, and Garnet started. It was the first sound she had heard in hours. Although it was broad daylight and the sun had risen well above the horizon, she shivered. It was uncanny, this silence. There was an eerie atmosphere in this place, as though someone had cast an evil spell over it.

She must get away from here. Reason told her that the silence could be no trick. Even Nicholas could not have kept such a large number of unruly Wreckers silent for so long. Something must have happened, something terrible and unaccountable. She was convinced that there was a curse on the house, and wished herself safely far away. Oh, if only she could be warm and secure in Cheveril Street again!

Slowly and deliberately she drew the bolt and unlocked the door of her chamber, then waited. Still no sound broke the hush. Her bundle under her arm, she crept stealthily out into the corridor, and glided silently towards the main staircase. Around her she could see the doors to other chambers standing open, and inside were signs of disorder, clothes lying strewn across bed and floors as though their owners had packed and left too hastily to care.

So something amiss had befallen to cause such an exodus. Stealth seemed unnecessary now, so Garnet walked boldly down the stairs, her swishing skirts the only sound in the unearthly stillness apart from the faint scuffing of her mules.

She flung open the door of the great hall. Again there were signs of disarray, spilt wine and overturned tables, cards on the floor, and the garish grotto that looked even tawdrier in the light of day. She slammed the door shut and made for the front entrance.

Suddenly she stiffened, tense with fear. From a chamber somewhere near her the sound of a heavy thump came to her ears as of a piece of furniture falling. Terror drove thoughts through her mind in rapid succession. Outside there would be no cover in which to hide until she reached distant trees; no horses or other means of quick escape remained; best to hide within the house until danger was over.

She burst through the nearest door, the one leading to the curio chamber, closed it quickly behind her and leaned on it, eyes closed and panting with fright.

When she opened her eyes again she found herself in semi-darkness, in which she could hear the thud of her own heartbeats. The curtains were still drawn across the tall windows, but in the twilight she could just distinguish the couch in the middle of the room. Her pounding heartbeat stopped. On the couch lay the figure of a man, and, unless she was mistaken, the man was Nicholas. So he had been lying in wait for her after all!

She was about to cry out in anger and disappointment when she noticed that he lay unnaturally still, and in a somewhat grotesque position. She put her fingers to her lips as if to stifle the cry, and tiptoed hesitantly towards him so as not to waken him if he were sleeping. He did not move.

She moved to the window and swished back the drapes gently. When she turned, she saw to her horror that his eyes were on her, silently watching.

"Nicholas," she said, a note of question in her voice. He did not reply. "Nicholas, are you well?" Still no answer came. She crept closer.

He lay sprawled on the couch in a strange, abandoned manner, like a rag doll whose stuffing had been pulled out, his limbs twisted around uncomfortably. His face was flushed and spotted with scarlet pinpricks.

"Nicholas, speak to me! Are you ill?" She could hear the rising note in her own voice betraying her fear. Was he too bewitched, under the spell of some evil influence? Was that the reason why all the other guests had fled?

Nicholas was straining, trying to utter something she could not catch. All that issued from his throat was a peculiar gurgling sound. Had he been wounded in a duel, perchance? He had no sign of injury that she could see, no trace of blood from a wound.

She straightened his twisted arms and legs and made him more comfortable, and all the while his clouded eyes watched her. As she surveyed him, his mouth jerked suddenly open again and a white-furred, swollen tongue protruded limply. Froth began to gather about his lips, and his face turned from red to a deep and angry purple.

Garnet was alarmed. He needed a physician, for he was undoubtedly very ill. But how could she find a physician, lost as she was in this unknown countryside? There were no servants to dispatch nor horses to ride in search of help.

Then at last he moved, a slow, painful effort that seemed to change gradually into a series of uncontrolled jerks and contortions. Within moments he was writhing and clutching at the covering of the couch, digging his fingernails deep into the silk and pulling its threads loose.

"Nicholas, tell me what to do! Where can I find help?" Garnet cried, her tears beginning to flow because she felt so useless and unable to help.

He could not answer her, dancing about uncontrollably as he was, like a creature possessed by a demon. His eyes were glaring angrily and squinting violently. His face was contorted into what seemed like an ugly smile. He was a terrible sight to behold, and Garnet was terrified.

And then suddenly the convulsion ceased. He fell back limply on the couch, and a hideous rattle came out from his throat, a long-drawn-out sound like an exhaled sigh, and then he lay silent, his eyes still open and staring. Garnet bent over him and could scarcely see him for her tears of fright.

He did not move again. His eyes were glazing, and Garnet realised he was no longer breathing. He was dead.

She knelt on the floor beside the couch, unable to believe it. She was too stunned by the unexpectedness of his death to be able to take it in. She had seen illness before, but not death at such close quarters, and it seemed too hideous to be true.

Illness one could accept and cope with, as on the occasion little Daniel had been so sick the physician had surrendered his fate to her. And as she thought of Daniel's illness it occurred to her that she had seen this same twitching of the face and the squint before, on that occasion. Nicholas had borne much the same signs as Daniel, even to the high fever and the angry red spots. The doctor had been unable to name Daniel's fever, a strange foreign one, he had said.

186

Was it possible Nicholas had not been under a spell, but had contracted the same contagion as Daniel? It seemed odd that two people in her life, both widely separated, should have caught the same rare fever. One could almost believe that she herself had brought the evil, first to one house, then to the other. She shuddered at the thought.

Was it possible she was the evil-doer? Did she carry some malevolent spell unknown to herself, to harm those she came near? Or had she warded off the spell from Daniel by her prayers and nursing, only to pass it on to Nicholas, to whom she wished harm? The thought of possibly being an unwitting witch terrified Garnet even more than Nicholas's ugly death. The penalty for witchery was death.

She looked up from her kneeling position and caught sight of Nicholas's hand, the fingers still enmeshed in the threads of the brocade couch. Fear rose in her throat. That was it! The rose brocade, that was the evil token she carried, the cause of all the misfortune. The remnant she had taken with her everywhere since she had left Madame Barin, that was the malefic influence. She must throw it away at once, nay, destroy it better, for fear it would cause trouble for someone else. Never again would she carry the rose brocade with her!

As she rose to fetch her bundle she looked at Nicholas's inert figure. To think she had caused a man's death through her own doing! A flicker of memory grew into a clear vision —she remembered the gypsy girl in Lady Caroline's apartments in Whitehall. "You will one day cause the death of the man who desires you, mistress," she had foretold. Garnet looked dispassionately at Nicholas's body. That was yet another prediction which had come to pass. And all because of her ambition to possess rose brocade. She felt sick with disgust and self-loathing.

Clattering hoofbeats broke Garnet's preoccupation. Someone was outside the house! She hastened to the door and heard a voice cry out.

"Garnet? Garnet, where are you?"

187

It was Matthew. Dear, dependable Matthew! She flung open the door. "I am here, Matthew!"

He rushed into the chamber, flushed and anxious. He flung his arms about her and held her close to him. "Thank God, Garnet! Thank God! I feared you might be dead," he said in a strange, cracked voice and burying his face in her shoulder. Garnet felt suddenly warm and alive. Someone cared for her safety, and enough to follow her all this way, too. She clung close to him for a minute.

"Thank heaven you came, Matthew. I am so happy to see you." They were feeble words, totally inadequate, but how else could she express her joy and relief at seeing him?

"You are unharmed?" He held her at arm's length to inspect her. "That swine did not touch you?"

"I am well," she answered calmly. "Nicholas is dead." She indicated the body on the couch. Matthew only glanced at him, then back to her.

"I must get you away from here, from this pestilential house," he muttered.

"How did you trace me, Matthew?" Garnet's numbed mind was beginning to function again.

"Daniel described the coach in which you were abducted. He said it had pussies on the door."

Garnet laughed, despite the tension and chill of this unpleasant house. "Dear Daniel, how I have missed him," she murmured.

"And he you, Garnet." Matthew hesitated a moment, then went on. "Garnet, we have both missed you desperately. You will come back to Cheveril Street, will you not?" He saw her gaze fall. "Not to stay, if you do not wish it, but at least for a time. And if you would consider it, we should like you to stay for always. Garnet, we love you, Daniel and I."

Garnet broke away from his arms. She did not deserve the love and faithfulness of this man and his son, and felt sick with shame, for above all else she would rather go back with him. But how could she, after having treated him so?

Matthew was watching her closely. "You would prefer to return to Whitehall?" he asked, and she could hear the disappointment in his voice.

"No, Matthew."

"Then you have other plans?"

"No, Matthew."

His face registered relief. "Then there is nothing to prevent you from coming to Cheveril Street," he said triumphantly. "Come, let us waste no more time." He took her arm and turned to go.

"One moment more. There is something I must do," said Garnet. She picked up her bundle again and walked purposefully to the fireplace and poked the ashes. Not an ember remained. She turned to Matthew. "Can you make a light for me?" she asked him.

Matthew came forward and struck a flint unquestioningly. He set fire to some paper in the hearth. Garnet unfastened her bundle and withdrew the remnant of rose brocade. This time she did not cradle it lovingly to her, but rather took it by the corner with her fingertips and held it over the flame.

The silk brocade twisted and writhed, as in a death agony, and one by one she watched the minute embroidered rosebuds wither and vanish. When every last vestige of the brocade had disappeared, Garnet felt that a heavy load had been lifted from her.

She rose, satisfied. "There, that is done," she said softly, and taking up her bundle she faced Matthew. "Now I am ready to go home."

Matthew took her arm, a proud smile on his lips, and together they walked out of Yester Park to where the untethered horse stood quietly cropping grass on the lawn.